SCRATCHES

BY JOSHUA MARSELLA

Scratches

Any references to historical events, real people, or real places are used fictitiously. Names, characters, and places are products of the author's imagination.

First Edition May 2020

ISBN: 9798642086827

For Aryn,
Thank you for believing in me
and supporting my dream.

"Beyond the reach of human rage
A drop of hell, a touch of strange ..."
Stephen King, *The Gunslinger*

- One -

"Connor! Bring me another bud, will ya? This one is *piss* warm!" Janet yelled from the living room.

"Alright, just give me a minute!" The boy groaned with more than a hint of irritability. "Talk about bad timing!" he grumbled under his breath.

Right then, Connor was preoccupied with an arduous undertaking. He had thought up the idea to move his bedroom down into the basement earlier in the week. He'd spotted a large space in the corner while he was bringing his mother's basket of laundry down to the washing machine. A majority of the abandoned junk in the basement had been emptied out before they'd moved in as requested by his mother.

After Connor promised her she would have no involvement, it didn't take much to convince her to allow him to move down there. It meant he would be out of her hair most of the time with his growingly agitated pubescent attitude. He foresaw the benefit of having a bigger living space compared to his current bedroom in addition to the increased privacy. It was also much cooler than his south facing bedroom that had become unbearably hot during the July heat wave they were suffering through. Whenever he complained about the heat his mother felt inclined to remind him that they couldn't afford an air conditioner nor the increased rates on the electric bill that came with the comfort from running one.

When Janet had called out the untimely request, he was in the process of moving his heavy dresser down the creaky wooden stairs alone. In spite of the fact he had removed the drawers and the few secondhand garments he owned beforehand, the roughed up piece of furniture was hefty and awkward to move. The bottom of the dresser made a loud thumping noise as it dropped onto each tread which unbeknownst to Connor had begun to aggravate his mother. For some unknown reason she avoided the basement like the plague. This was why he always did her laundry. She had included the task on his list of summer chores to help her out while he was on school break.

"Please hurry! The commercial's almost over!" Janet barked from her reclined position in the ragged faux leather recliner as she chugged down the last few sips of her room temperature beer with a wince. Warm beer was her least favorite kind, but she wouldn't let a drop go to waste. This was her nightly vegging ritual. Janet regularly worked a long shift behind the cash register at the convenience store on the edge of town just off the turnpike. Burnchester Beverage was a combination gas station and liquor store where all the town drunks would stop on their way home from work to pick up that night's drink of choice.

THUD   THUD   THUD

Finally after much effort, Connor reached the patch of old carpet that had been placed on the cement floor at the bottom of the stairwell. Through his pink pursed lips, he exhaled a deep sigh of relief knowing the remainder of the move would be a piece of cake in comparison. Connor hadn't had a paternal figure during his entire twelve years of life and usually wasn't bothered by it. This was one of those few errands where he knew a father would come in handy. He often wondered about his father but hadn't gathered the guts to ask his mother about him again. Not since career week at school a few years ago. Curiosity got the better of him and when he asked her what his father did for a living she erupted with indignation. He sensed her resentment towards the man so he decided to just let it go entirely. Janet could get vicious when she lost her temper. Even more so if she'd been drinking.

As he inhaled Connor was struck by the scent he identified as 'old basement smell'. Lifting his skinny arm, he tucked his shoulder length hair back behind his ear and out of his face. Though they shared a similar shade of dark brown that matched their eyes, his mother's hair was much longer and grazed the bottom of her shoulder blades.

Before he finished the move, he hurriedly bolted upstairs to bring his mother the cold refill she had requested. This was a chore he was all too familiar with, yet nonetheless found abhorrent considering how close she was sitting to the yellow Maytag refrigerator. The house, furniture and a majority of the appliances were part of an inheritance. An inheritance Janet begrudgingly accepted after her father's untimely death.

As he walked through the living room and into the kitchen, he heard the familiar voice of Pat Sajak calling out to Vannah White to ask her if there was an R on the board. A clear indication that the commercials were over which would likely increase his mother's irritability.

"I'm here. I'm here." he reassured her.

There were only three beers left in the 12-pack box she brought home from work that evening. A feeling of shame came over him as he noticed the fridge was nearly empty minus a few condiments and a half gallon of expired milk. This meant he would have to scrounge for his dinner like a wild animal. Connor grabbed one of the cold cans, shut the fridge, and proceeded to deliver it to his mother.

Their 13" Panasonic television had her undivided attention, but Janet still managed to reach out and snatch the beer from Connor's bony grip. The can made a sharp hiss as she popped the top.

"Well thank you so much!" She spoke in a sarcastic tone. "But it took you long enough *didn't it?* Commercial's already over! What the hell were you doing down there anyways? You're causing such a raucous I can barely hear the television!" Her speech had begun to slur with drunken annoyance. A feeling she had grown accustomed to daily since they moved into that house.

Connor rolled his eyes since he knew his mother wouldn't bother to turn her attention from the game show to hear his response.

"I *told* you last week I was going to move my room to the basement. It's way cooler down there and my room feels like a sauna. I can't open my window because the screen is missing. The damn mosquitos will eat me alive one of these nights *if* I don't die of heat stroke first!" He stretched his arms out to the side overdramatically like he was reenacting a crucifixion. He assumed correctly. She hadn't bothered to look up at her son once to address him.

"Well hurry it up *will* ya? That heavy banging is giving me a headache and I have to work a dub tomorrow." She shook her fisted beer at the TV spilling a few drops onto the carpet without a care. "Ask for a T you idiot! I swear they find the biggest *dumbasses* to come on this show!"

Feeling ignored, Connor pivoted to return to his former bedroom so he could finish picking up the remainder of his few scattered belongings. Without looking back he addressed her concern.

"I'm finished with all the heavy lifting. Just got a few more small things to bring down. I'll be quiet for the rest of the night. You won't hear a peep from me." He moved his fingers across his mouth in a zipping gesture that his mother didn't see.

"That's good. Thanks Connie!" She raised the beer to her brow in a mock salute.

Connor despised that nickname, but it was better than the colorful names she conjured up when she was in a bad mood or drunk off her ass. The latter was more often the case than not since moving in. He couldn't recall whether his mother drank so much in their old apartment. He supposed the lack of a house payment permitted her more spending money. Still, it didn't make much sense for her to just start drinking in excess for seemingly no reason. The bit of extra cash obviously didn't go towards keeping the refrigerator stocked with food. Connor's constantly growling stomach reminded him of that almost daily.

Part of him was convinced his mother didn't feel comfortable living back in her childhood home. But he also knew the alternative was far worse. She despised her parents and he rightfully assumed the constant reminders of her childhood were difficult for her to handle. Similar to the subject of *his* father, she downright refused to discuss her parents. She'd provided just enough specifics for him to appreciate how deep seated her hatred was. Connor became accepting of the fact that his mother was a woman with many secrets. But in no way did that indicate he was

Joshua Marsella

willing to give up his quest for answers to his innumerable questions.

- Two -

By nine that evening his room was mostly set up the way he wanted it. After several grueling hours of heavy lifting down the stairs, he had managed to relocate his furniture to the spot he chose in the corner of the dank basement. The only tasks that remained were to place his bedding on his twin mattress and to hang some old sheets he found. He hung them up around the room with thumb tacks for make-shift walls to make him feel less exposed even though they were scattered with small tears from years of use. He was aware that his mother wasn't likely to ever go down there, but it still made him feel better to have them up. It didn't take long for him to notice that the basement had an eerie atmosphere once the overhead lights were turned off. The 60 watt bulb that was housed in his bedside lamp didn't put out much light, but it was all he had.

On the opposite side of the stairwell was an old nightlight resembling a lantern that was plugged in just above the washing machine. The tiny yellowish bulb put out just enough light for him to navigate his way up the stairs without tripping in case he needed to use the bathroom at night. Connor felt impressed with his new digs so he laid down on his bed to read one of his favorite comic books before passing out.

Although he was physically comfortable, neither the hanging sheet walls nor the latest edition of "Tales From The Crypt" he was reading helped him shake the eerie feeling of being watched. He tucked himself under his blanket to reduce his exposure before finishing the final few pages. Like most kids, something about having his feet under a blanket made him feel safer which helped him relax.

Connor loved anything horror. Movies, comics, posters, rumored haunted houses. He enjoyed the rush of adrenaline he felt while thinking about things that go bump in the night. The fictional tales of monsters, ghosts, and the walking dead somehow made him feel better about his benign existence. No matter how bad he felt things were, at least he knew he wouldn't be gutted by a raging werewolf or have his blood drained by a centuries old vampire. Truth was he'd always had a fondness for spooky imagery as long as those images stayed on the pages of his cartoonish comic books or on the TV screen.

- Three -

The house was in a state of disrepair after years of neglect by Janet's father George. He had built it on a cheap piece of property that was approximately twenty-five feet away from an aging cemetery that had a rusted chain-link fence surrounding its perimeter. By no coincidence, it was the same cemetery that later harbored the coffin containing his battered and rotting corpse. He was laid to rest in a modified position of attention with his arms laying across his chest as opposed to laying at his sides like a proper marine.

Connor was thrilled when his mother told him they were moving into her childhood home after his grandfather had passed away under mysterious circumstances. This would be the first real house he'd ever lived in. He had never met his grandfather and didn't know much about him. They didn't have any pictures of his grandparents nor did they hold a viewing prior to his burial so he didn't even know what he looked like. The sealed coffin that he saw as he peeked through a window on the day of his burial was the closest he had ever come to a proper introduction. Although he had heard enough from his mother to know he didn't care to meet the man.

Even though Janet didn't seem excited, she was at least happy that they were moving out of the rundown two bedroom apartment in the city where they had been living for most of her son's life. The apartment building's hallways smelled like marijuana or urine. People were always slamming doors or yelling at each other. Their flat had walls that were paper thin and only one window that could open. All that being said, the rent was cheap and it was all his mother could afford on her minimum wage income from the store.

Janet hated her father and with good reason. He was an angry abusive drunk who used to beat her on a regular basis for seemingly no reason at all but the pleasure of it. Her mother wasn't innocent either since she apparently got fed up with his behavior and abandoned them both. When Janet had nowhere else to go, having no other family to advocate for her, she was forced to live alone with her father. Eventually she herself ran away from home before graduating high school which made it difficult for Janet to find a good-paying job. She gave up the search once she finally got hired at the store which gave her just enough income to get by. She always talked about getting her G.E.D. but raising a child by herself plus working a full time dead end job proved to be more than enough work. Free time wasn't a benefit that was granted to many single mothers.

Connor's deductive reasoning told him that the stress and trauma that followed her from childhood was likely why she drank so much and had a hard time staying in a steady relationship. Part of him felt sorry for his mother knowing some of the abuse she endured for so long. Another part of him resented the way she had chosen to keep the cycle of poor parenting going. Still, sometimes he thought maybe it wasn't entirely her fault and he should try to cut her some slack.

- Four -

One freezing cold night in late November of the previous year, George was on a bender when the furnace decided to go on the fritz. He was relaxing on the couch watching an old *M*A*S*H* rerun he had seen a thousand times before. Per usual, he was wearing only his underwear and drinking Jack Daniels straight in a stubby glass. Had he not been so liquored up he might have noticed the goosebumps that covered his sagging flesh. Like most older people he kept the thermostat set around 75 degrees so he eventually took notice of the sudden drop in temperature when chalky puffs of booze scented breath escaped his mouth as he exhaled. The God damned furnace must have broken down again.

Angrily he gulped the last sip, set his glass on the coffee table in front of him and slowly stood up off the couch wobbling at the hips. His knees popped like they were filled with kernels of popcorn. His feet felt as heavy as cinder blocks while he ventured down the hallway. He bumped into the wall several times before he reached the door to the cellar. He was determined to make it down to check on the furnace regardless of his current condition

knowing he'd likely freeze to death if he didn't. Standing
in the doorway of the cellar, his head was spinning in a
drunken haze. He started to feel unsure of himself as he
gazed down the steep wooden steps though his uncertainty
was short lived. As George took the first step, he
miscalculated and the heel of his foot slipped off the edge
of the first stair tread and he tumbled down the rest of the
way.

*   *   *

George didn't regularly receive much mail, so it took
over two weeks before the carrier became suspicious
seeing the old man's few bills piled up uncollected in the
leaning box by the road. Nor was he known for taking
vacations or leaving town. The carrier contacted the
Burnchester Police Department to recommend they
perform a wellness check on the old man knowing he lived
alone. It could just be that the recent frigid temperatures
had kept the man indoors, but wellness checks were
common practice in the small town. The P.D. sent out a
patrol car later that same day without hesitation.

Officer Thomaston could sense something was amiss
as soon as he turned the unlocked door knob. He'd been

knocking loudly for several minutes in the early afternoon sun but had got no response. He was fairly new on the force so he was used to getting sent out to do menial tasks like wellness checks. He considered this just a step up from filling in for the parking enforcement officer. When he entered the kitchen he immediately felt that the temperature inside wasn't much warmer than outside. *Poor bastard didn't keep up on his heating bill* was his first thought.

He called out, "Police! Hello, Mr. Hanscott! This is Officer Thomaston from Burnchester P.D. Are you home? I'm just here to perform a wellness check, sir."

He could hear upbeat music softly playing from the living room. As he rounded the corner he jumped a little when he heard Rod Roddy's boisterous voice yelling "*TIM WENTLY! COME ON DOWN!*" He walked over and turned off the *The Price is Right* assuming the old man would be home if the television was on. Once the TV was quiet he was met with a dead silence that felt unnatural. He could see his breath as he called out to George a second time.

He continually attempted to make his presence known as not to startle the old war veteran in his home, still no response came. He turned, eyed several empty bottles of Jack Daniels littering the coffee table and the floor around the couch along with an empty drinking glass. The sight made him reminisce about the morning after high school party. The smells of stale booze, body odor and vomit emanating from the filthy carpet weren't far off in the memory of the young officer who never barely finished earning his diploma. But this was clearly the home of a man with a serious drinking problem, not a party house.

As he moved on to investigate further, he was almost immediately struck with a nauseating smell that quickly overpowered the nostalgia. The sickening odor became more dominant as he cautiously moved down the hallway. He cupped his hand over his nose and mouth which did little to nothing to shield his senses from the unidentified stench. Unsure of what he was going to come up against, he carefully reached down, removed the pistol from its holster with the safety still engaged.

His blood pressure rose slightly knowing if the old man popped out from one of the bedrooms and spotted an unexpected guest holding a firearm, there could be unintended trouble. The overwhelming stench that permeated down the corridor combined with his gut instincts reassured him that wasn't likely to happen. He saw a door open into the hallway. He was glad to see a light was on. *Maybe the old timer is down in the basement but just didn't hear me come in.* He thought to himself as a weak attempt to calm his nerves. To avoid any surprises he called out one final time.

When no response came a familiar feeling of dread came over him considering this wasn't his first wellness check. He knew what was next. A body, a phone call, hours of paperwork. Few things cops hated more than paperwork. As he reached the open doorway, the top step came into view. He looked down and gasped as he discovered the source of the offensive odor.

"Damn George! What the hell did you do man?" He spoke aloud in a somber tone knowing for certain that he was alone.

- Five -

Several weeks of investigation later, the authorities finally tracked down the dead's only next of kin. Janet was surprised when she received a visit from the local sheriff to tell her the news, though she wasn't the slightest bit heartbroken. She knew this day would come sooner or later. A heavy sense of relief swept over her. After a few days of calling around, she decided it was most befitting to have him buried in the cemetery that was neighboring the house that he built by himself after he returned home from his deployment in Vietnam. But mainly because Veterans Affairs refused to accept responsibility for his body. She loathed the dead man and just wanted to be sure he was finally underground where he could cause her no more harm.

Janet decided not to waste a dime on a formal funeral so the unceremonious burial took place that following April once the ground was fully thawed. Her and Connor moved into the house a couple weeks later once the details of the will were sorted out with a probate attorney. A pastor from the local Methodist church as well as two gravediggers were the only people in attendance at the burial since Janet had refused to write an obituary notifying the public of his demise. Connor watched from a window while his mother casually strolled over to the cemetery after the hasty ceremony. She generously helped the gravediggers by kicking some of the dirt from the pile into the hole if for no other reason than to confirm the bastard was truly soon-to-be wormfood. Since then, the only visitors to his grave had been the caretakers who maintained the grounds. Even though the gravesite was within a stone's throw of the house, Janet never made an attempt to visit her father's final resting place again. Never said a prayer for his salvation. Her father had been dead to her for a very long time.

- Six -

Connor liked his new basement bedroom much more than his upstairs one, but he still had a hard time getting used to the unpleasant smells. When he would spend time down there in the evenings he would casually sneak away a few sticks of his mother's incense to burn to help mask the damp, mildew smell. He taped up a couple of posters of his favorite horror movies he had picked up for cheap at a thrift store. *Pet Sematary*, *Hellraiser* and *Friday the 13th* oddly made him feel right at home. He used an old stained dish rag to cover over the small rectangular window that was level with the ground outside facing the cemetery. It wasn't the Ritz Carlton, but it had started to feel like home after the first week or so. As he looked around his room he thought to himself, *maybe this could work. Maybe this house wasn't all that bad.*

He was a fairly light sleeper so any soft noise was almost guaranteed to wake him up out of his slumber. One Saturday night, he had stayed up late to watch his favorite show *Are You Afraid of the Dark?* Janet worked the night shift so she wouldn't be home until after one the next morning once she closed down the store. When the show was over he shut off the television, grabbed a drink of water, then walked down the creaky wooden stairs to his room. He grazed his hand against the wall for added support when his fingers noticed something odd. There were four deep gashes running down the wall a short ways. He wondered if those had that been there before? He didn't remember having done that when he was moving the furniture. The wet earthy smell was more potent this evening which he attributed to the heavy rain that had fallen earlier that day. The swift change in temperature plus the cold cement under his feet made him shiver. He wished he hadn't kicked off his socks while laying on the couch. He turned on the bedside lamp, disappointed to see he had no more incense sitting beside the tinfoil burner. He leaned back onto his pillow and picked up the comic book that laid on his bed. The cool air helped lower his core temperature so he didn't bother to crawl under the comforter. It felt good on his skin. After less than 20 minutes his copy of *Creepshow* fell out of his hands, landed on his chest and he was sound asleep.

A couple hours later Connor was in a deep sleep before he was abruptly awakened by an ear-piercing scratching noise coming from somewhere in the darkness beyond the tattered sheets.

SCRAAATCH   SCRAAATCH   SCRAAATCH

First he thought it was part of his dream but once the rotten, sour smell infiltrated his nostrils he knew he was awake. He opened his eyes to darkness, quickly sat up in bed knocking his comic book onto the floor. The scratches faded away leading him to believe that he was just hearing things. There was surely some logical explanation for the noise. His eyes started to adjust to the dark just as he reached out to turn on his lamp giving himself a better look around the room. He laid his head back down on the pillow, stared up at the ceiling for what felt like an hour and listened intently. As the sleepiness crept back he decided to keep his lamp on the remainder of the night. Around 1:30 in the morning he finally nodded off after he heard his mother come home from work.

Upstairs, Janet quietly pulled open the fridge door to drop off the twelve-pack of beer she brought home. She tore open the box, hauled out a cold one, popped the tab and chugged it down to celebrate the end of her lengthy shift. She tossed the empty into the sink then grabbed a second beer to bring into bed with her. "One for the road," she gleefully whispered to herself with no shame.

The house felt almost abandoned with Connor's room now being in the basement. She had sometimes liked to peek in at him while he slept soundly like she would when he was a baby. Her boy looked so sweet and innocent. Now unsure whether it was nostalgia or the buzz from the beer she pounded, a slight wave of sorrow rushed over her as she thought about how quickly he was growing up. He seemed to want nothing to do with her which she hoped was just a phase. She knew that painful feeling of a loveless childhood.

As lonely as she felt now, once he moved out to start his own life she would truly be alone. Janet was unable to reassure herself that he would come home to visit his mother once he had a family of his own.

Something inside her compelled her to fight the maternal urge to form a lasting bond with her son. Perhaps this was a common feeling among young mothers whose children unintentionally robbed them of their youth. Regardless it was her emotion to deal with but Connor would pay the price.

Janet crept into her dark room, slipped into a nightgown and crawled under the covers without opening the road soda. She no longer felt self-congratulatory. She felt remorse.

Shortly after the sleep came, her closet door began to slide open. Heavy lascivious breaths released an obnoxious odor from the gaping rot mouth of the figure that stood erect in the darkness to watch the mother sleep.

- Seven -

The next few nights went on without any strange happenings. His mother was working the day shift the rest of the week so Connor spent more time in his room after dinner. Once in a while he would sit at the kitchen table where the light was good to sketch characters from his comic books. Zombies, bloody hands, severed heads, and other gory images that piqued his interest. Janet *always* held a claim to the t.v. when she was home from work. Local news, Wheel of Fortune then Jeopardy. She didn't care for much else considering they only had access to the basic cable channels. This didn't really bother Connor since he preferred reading over t.v. anyways unless there was a scary movie showing.

After he finished his reading his last comic on a rainy Thursday evening around 9pm, Connor wasn't quite tired yet. He turned on his clock radio and decided to get caught up on the hit songs with the *High-Five at Nine*. Once he laid back onto his pillow to listen it didn't take long before his eyelids felt heavy as sandbags. Since he had nothing better to do he welcomed the sleep. As he slept to the sounds of pop music the radio started to put out a static while the red station indicator slowly slid itself up the dial. Eventually it stopped itself on a classic rock station.

The static cleared as John Fogerty's raspy vocals and upbeat guitar played over the airwaves. The singer belted out *Bad Moon Rising* through the tiny speakers beside Connor's bed. Then just as before, the sound of scratches started up somewhere in the darkness. This time it was considerably louder and more aggressive. It sounded like roofing nails tearing into a chalkboard which made Connor grit his teeth and cringe.

SCRAAAATCH SCRAAAAATCH SCRAAAATCH

Connor peeled open his eyes which abruptly ended his deep sleep making him feel disoriented. He lifted his head up off the pillow, rubbed the crust from his eyelids, then squinted looking out towards the sheets. His eyes were adjusted to the low light so he could just make out the silhouette of a dark figure that stood behind the sheet in the distant yellow hue of the nightlight.

He snapped out of his confusion but moved onto a state of shock. This was no dream. He was no longer alone. There was a person or a thing in the basement with him. He felt the malevolent presence of the figure as his state of shock quickly shifted to fear.

Fogerty continued to belt out his dire warning as Connor tossed aside the covers in a panic. He swung his legs out of the bed letting them dangle over the edge. His instincts told him to stand up and run out of there but he had nowhere to go. His path was blocked. He was so discombobulated he hardly noticed the scratching stopped.

Light. He needed light. He leaned over and reached for his lamp so hastily he knocked it down before he could turn it on. Terror-stricken, he stood the lamp back up then found the knob. The light shocked his senses as he turned back around toward the figure but it was no longer visible. He cocked his head to listen for footsteps but heard none. He scooted forward dropping his bare feet onto the chilly cement.

Hesitantly, he crept his way toward the small gap between the hanging sheets. His heart nearly beat itself out of his chest like a war drum. He yanked back the sheet to reveal nothing but the dimly lit space. Unaware that his breathing had slowed down he exhaled with a deep sigh of relief. As he inhaled through his nose he caught a strong whiff of stagnant booze and a pungent sour smell he couldn't identify. It reminded him of expired milk. He wondered if his mother had come down while he slept but that made no sense. She often had a similar smell after her nights of heavy drinking but he knew that it couldn't possibly be her. If she wouldn't go down there in the daytime there's no way she would come down in the darkness of the night.

As Fogerty sang the final chorus, Connor let go of the sheet, walked back to his nightstand and turned off the radio with an audible click. The silence in the room was deafening. He considered waking up his mother but didn't know if she'd crawled back in from her shift yet. He hopped back into bed under the assumption that his overtired mind just played a cruel trick on him. The image of the figure behind the sheet chilled him to the bone. He pulled the covers up to his chin deciding to sleep with the lamp on again. The sense that he was being watched was an inescapable feeling. He turned the radio back on to help distract his mind. The radio DJ announced the next song but Connor was too distracted to notice the station had changed by itself. He stared at the ceiling as Janis Joplin crooned out *Summertime* over a grungy, psychedelic lead guitar which put the icing on the creepy cake.

- Eight -

Connor knew the house's history was a touchy subject for his mother so he didn't like to ask many questions about it. He was thankful to be living there. Even more thankful to be out of their old apartment. But after the unexplainable phenomena in the basement he felt at least few questions were warranted. Something peculiar was taking place in this house. Something he couldn't deny after what he saw.

The next morning while he leaned over a bowl of soggy corn flakes at the kitchen table, he decided to take a chance. Janet stared at the coffee maker waiting for the slow drip to fill up the glass carafe just enough to pour herself a cup. Bent over the counter, her chin rested in her hands as she fought off a throbbing hangover like she did most mornings.

When Connor glanced up at her, his attention was drawn to a series of red swollen scratches on her shoulder blade. He felt uncomfortable questioning her about them, but was still first to interrupt the silence.

"Mom, do you by chance remember anything weird ever happening to you in this house when you were a little girl?"

Janet's heart skipped a beat at the abrupt question. "What do you mean by weird exactly?" her tone carried a tinge of suspicion.

"I don't know. Did you ever see something you couldn't explain? Like maybe a looming presence or strange noises?" Connor asked but sounded unsure of himself.

"Not that I recall. Though it wasn't such an old house when I was a girl. The cemetery always creeped me out though. Kids tend to have very vivid imaginations. I was no different."

"Well, do you happen to know how grandpa died? You've never really talked about it." He felt the familiar sense of regret he always felt after each mention of his grandfather. He knew it wouldn't make her happy.

Janet tipped her head back and sighed dramatically as if he broke her deep train of thought. "That's because you know I don't like to talk about him. He was a terrible person. I wanted him to have nothing to do with us! That's why I made sure you never met him. I know he hated me for it, but I didn't give a shit!"

"No, I know. I understand that much. That's not why I am asking though. I'm only wondering because strange things have been happening in the basement at night." He paused for a reaction, but got none. "Sometimes when I'm down there I get the feeling I am being watched. It feels like someone or something is prying in on me from the darkness. Then other times there's a bad smell-"

This got Janet's attention. She turned her head to the side so one eye could look towards her son.

"Well first off, all basements smell funny. It's almost like an unwritten rule or something. Secondly, you shouldn't watch those scary shows before bed when I'm not home. They put ideas in your head that you get all creeped out when nothing is really there. I'm sure your addiction to those horror comics you insist on reading before bed doesn't help either! You tend to have a very overactive imagination." She turned back around and poured herself a cup of Folgers.

"No, it's not that! I know the difference. I love those shows and comics *because* I'm not easily scared. That feeling I get when I'm down there almost makes me sick to my stomach." The memory of the dark figure silhouetted on the sheet sent a chill down his spine. "Did they even tell you how he died?"

"Yes, of course they told me, but I don't feel it's necessarily any of your business nor is it relevant. Especially since-" She paused mid sentence then continued. "It's just not, okay? People die, that's life. He was old and lived an unhealthy lifestyle." She took a slow sip off her cup. "This is a decent enough house. We are lucky to be out of that shitty apartment. I know you have to agree with me." She counts off with her fingers. "We have no mortgage, the car is a beater but it's paid off, and the neighbors are quiet. Most of the time." She looks at her son and winks with a sly smirk on her face to emphasize that she made a joke. Connor played along shooting her a smile, but his concerns were not resolved and his questions remained unanswered.

She continued, "I was worried about this when you decided to move your room down there. *All* basements are creepy to some extent. Not to mention living so close to a cemetery probably doesn't help either. But I assure you, it's completely safe." She topped off her mug and indulged herself in the bitter goodness of the black coffee.

Connor stirred at the last few corn flakes that floated around in the milk with his spoon. "Nevermind, it's fine. Maybe you're right. I'll take a break from the horror comics for a while to see if that helps. Except, it's more than just the feeling of being watched or the gross smells. I woke up the other night and heard a loud scratching noise coming from somewhere down there. Like, on the floor or the foundation. Do you think we have mice?"

"It's an old house Connie, I wouldn't be surprised if we have a few mice. Maybe even a squirrel found its way in to avoid the heat. It's most likely you were probably dreaming. Dreams can feel real sometimes. Like you're really there until you wake up feeling confused or dazed before you realize you're in bed. It happens to me all the time." She felt good about her answer and hoped to God that would be the end of the inquisition.

"Of course I know that, but it *wasn't* just the scratching. I actually saw someone too. Or some*thing*. You wouldn't know this, but there's an old nightlight down there by the washing machine. I could see what looked like a person standing on the other side of the sheets I hung up for walls. A tall figure. Well, a shadow at least. Just standing there like a statue. I didn't know if you had a guest over or something, but that didn't make any sense. I knew it couldn't be you because you *refuse* to go down there, which I still don't understand."

Janet dropped her coffee spoon onto the floor which made a loud clang startling Connor. She bent down to pick it up, rinsed it off and her tone was quickly changed to one of agitation. "You were just dreaming! End of this discussion! There was no one in the house. You know I haven't even been on a date in years, let alone have a man in this house." She sounded embarrassed. "I'm telling you, it was your imagination playing tricks on you. Horror movies and dark cellars are a perfect recipe for the heebie jeebies. Just promise me you'll take a break from the scary stuff for a while. Read some fantasy comics or those Spiderboy ones. Or how about you read an actual *book* for once, God forbid!"

Connor privately scoffed at her hypocrisy. He had never seen his mother with a book in her hand unless it was the *TV Guide*.

"It's Spider-*Man*." He corrected her with an edge to his tone. "That stuff always bores the heck out of me, but I guess I'll give it a try. Not sure how it'll help, but I suppose it can't hurt."

"Whatever it is, just *no more* scary stuff! At least for a while. And no more of those shows either. Watch some *Full House* or *The Brady Bunch*. I always liked that one. I'm going to be working a lot this week putting in some extra hours. I *don't* want to have to worry about you being creeped out all the time. Deal?"

"Alright, alright."

"No more talking about that wretched beast of a man either. He's not worth your time or mine. He's dead and buried. We are lucky to have this house no matter the circumstances with which we got it. Agreed?"

"Agreed." he replied without conviction. He didn't want to push her buttons, but he had another question. He stood up from the table then walked to the sink. "Just one more question. I promise. Was your father a heavy drinker?"

She picked up her cup of coffee, started to exit the kitchen but stopped before she did. With her back to him she asked, "What would make you ask me that?" This time she sounded offended. She wondered whether he implied something due to her increased drinking the past few weeks, then she left the room.

"Nevermind. I'm sorry. No more questions." He removed the empty beer cans from the sink then stacked them on the counter so he could wash out his cereal bowl. When he finished he was surprised to see Janet return to the kitchen to slap a ten dollar bill on the table.

"Here. Go buy yourself a couple of comic books that *aren't* scary with that. Get out of the house. Go explore the town. Make some friends for God's sake. It's supposed to be decent out today. Try to enjoy the summer while it's still here." She hoped that the money would be the end of it.

He dried his hands on the towel hanging from the cabinet beneath the sink, swiped up the wrinkled bill and slid it into his back pocket. He had a feeling she was hiding something from him, but this would somewhat make up for it. Maybe he *was* just creeped out by the comics. For the time being he will let his mother buy his silence.

"Thanks. I will."

- Nine -

Later that day, Connor took a ride downtown on his banana seat bicycle. The silver paint was chipped, the chain was rusty, tassels shot out from handlebars, but he loved that bicycle. It was his one source of pride.

His mother was right about the forecast. As he pedaled past the cemetery he noticed right away that the humidity wasn't so intense and a gentle breeze was blowing. The white clouds looked like soft cotton against the deep blue sky. This made for a welcome change from the gloomy basement he had grown accustomed to. The sun reflected brightly off his chalky pale skin which looked unnatural on a kid in the summer. The fresh air almost tasted sweet on his tongue. His lungs seemed to thank him for the recess from the stagnant basement.

This wasn't a bad little town. The traffic was minimal so he was able to ride on the paved road for most of the trip with minimal risk.

Main Street was about two miles from his house. He was anxious to hit up *Downtown Comics & Tabletop Games* which had been his favorite store for quite some time. The shop was holed up inside an old brick building that was a part of the original downtown construction. The sidewalk was also made of bricks that were uneven and in dire need of replacement. He stopped outside the comic book store, leaned his bike up against the green light post hoping it would be there when he returned. He pushed open the screen door triggering a bell above his head to alert the overweight clerk that he had a patron.

The clerk set down his copy of *Daredevil Vol. 16* but didn't stand up from his tall wooden stool behind the counter. A small flimsy desk fan blew in his direction. The room had a smell that was reminiscent of a dusty old church. Around the shop he could see glass cases filled with paintable gaming miniatures, comic books and rare trading cards. The walls were littered with posters, cardboard cutouts of superheroes and other fantastical characters. They even had a cool suit of armor in the corner at the back of the shop. Connor felt like he could live in this place.

"Good afternoon, young sir! What can I do ya for?" The clerk asked cheerily. "Are you a comic guy or a gamer?" He asked before he wiped the side of his bristly face with a handkerchief. Although it was nice outside, the humidity in the old building was still noticeable. "Wait, don't tell me! You look like a reader. An *ed-gema-cated* man!"

Connor was less than impressed but he could see the man was well-intentioned. He had visited the shop at least a couple times a month for the past few years. His mother would drop him off when she would go grocery shopping in town where it was less crowded than the city market. Sometimes he would just browse, but other times he had a little spending money saved up in the off chance his mother gave him an allowance. "That's right! A comic guy. I'm looking for something cheap and of the super hero variety." The words made Connor die a little inside.

"Oh yeah, I've seen you in here a buncha times. You're normally a big horror fan aren't you? Is it *Tales from the Crypt*?" He raised his hands up to either side of his head, wiggled his fingers in a silly ghoulish fashion while attempting a poor imitation of the crypt keeper's screeching laugh.

"Yep, that's me alright. *Creepshow* too! Anything horror. Those are my absolute favorites! Still waiting on the latest edition to be available. Although, unfortunately my mother wants me to take a break from the horror for a bit." He looked down at the floor with an expression of embarrassment. "You know, you have a good memory for an old guy." Connor gave him a playful grin. A little sucking up couldn't hurt when bartering was involved.

The clerk returned a big toothy simper of his own. "Oh bummer man! Moms can be such-a-draaaag!" The man jived as an obvious bid to sound younger than 37, but failed miserably.

"Well, some weird stuff has been happening at my house that she thinks is just my *"overactive imagination"*." He mimicked his mother's voice while he made air quotes with his fingers. "I was hoping to pick up a couple Spider-Man comics or something cheesy like that." He sounded disappointed and abashed. That was kiddy stuff. He prefered the gore and the macabre.

The clerk shifted forward in his stool but remained seated. "Weird stuff you say?" Connor had clearly piqued his curiosity. "What sort of weird stuff?" He asked with genuine interest in his tone. "Sometimes *kid, parents just don't understand!* Jazzy Jeff and the Fresh Prince, 1988. Um... Probably too young for that one though. Ya know kid, maybe you could use an outsider's perspective. I'm a bit of an expert when it comes to the world of the unknown. Not to toot my own horn, but I've seen every episode of *Unsolved Mysteries*. Even memorized the hotline. 1-800-876-5353." He recalled in the best Robert Stack voice he could muster.

This made Connor chuckle. He instantly liked this guy. They had briefly met in passing when he bought comics but he'd never really talked to him. If his mom wouldn't listen to his concerns, maybe this guy could play the role of surrogate father figure and help ease his mind.

"Well it's probably nothing like my mom suspects, but I recently moved my bedroom into the basement of our house. It's much cooler down there. Anyways, some strange things happened a couple of nights this week that I can't really explain or ignore for that matter." He looked around to see if anyone else was in the shop, but it was just the two of them. He didn't want to sound like a loony person. "First it was just a feeling of being watched. You know what I mean? I really felt like something was in the darkness watching me."

"Ooooh I definitely know that feeling! Humans have some killer instincts man, or I guess it's called intuition. I've been playing a lot of Super Nintendo lately. *Killer Instincts,* great game! Anyways, I digress. Go on!"

The clerk wiped his wide forehead with his sweat saturated bandana. "The name's Jeff by the way! Pleasure to formally meet ya even though I've seen ya in here a lot. You're what we call a 'regular'."

"Connor. Nice to meet you too." He gave him an awkward half wave to avoid having to shake his big, sweaty mitt. "So as I was saying-"

Connor proceeded to tell Jeff about the scratching, the smells, the dark figure and the clock radio.

"See, my grandfather was a *really* bad dude. My mother refuses to talk about him. After he died, we inherited his house. After what's been happening I can't help but think that this weird stuff going on and his death are somehow connected. I can feel the negative energy in the house, especially when I am home alone. Did I mention we live right next to this creepy old cemetery where-" Jeff cut him off mid sentence.

"Wait a minute. Where did you say you live?" Jeff rubbed his thumb and index finger on his cleft chin as if he was concentrating really hard. It made a rough, scratchy noise on the bristles like a cat's tongue.

"Well I didn't say, actually. It's the older somewhat rundown house out on Thomas Hill Road, right beside the old cemetery. My grandfather built the place in the 60's or something. Now I live there with my mom, just the two of us."

"Did you say Thomas-Hill-Road? The old cemetery? Was that late last year when he died? Small town, ya know? It was kind of the gossip on the streets for a few days. Oh, um- Sorry for your loss by the way."

"Thanks, and yes. It's fine though. I never met the guy." Connor said as he shrugged his shoulders. "Like I said, my mom told me he was a real a-hole. I won't get into details, but mostly because I don't have any."

"Okay, okay. I do remember hearing about that. Officer Thomaston, the cop that did the wellness check on him is a regular here. He fancies himself a *Justice League* fan. Kind of cliché if you ask me, but he's a nice enough guy. Gives us a lot of business. Anyways, after the news broke about your grandpa dying I overheard him telling the owner of this shop what had happened. He was pretty shook up about it. Guess he needed someone to talk to. They're second cousins or something like that. Cheaper than a therapist I suppose."

"*Really?* Do you remember any of what he said?" Connor moved closer to the counter with a hint of desperation in his eyes.

Jeff hesitated then eyed Connor with a look of slight concern. He continued "I didn't hear all of the conversation. Just enough to satisfy my morbid sense of curiosity. I also like horror comics sometimes but mostly movies. Anyways, I heard him say something about finding your grandfather lying at the bottom of the basement stairs in nothing but his crusty whitey tighties. Unfortunately he had been lying there for a couple of weeks. Deceased. Broken bones, blood, a real mess. He was starting to decay by the time he was discovered."

"Jesus... Well, what happened to him? Did he have a heart attack or something?" Connor seemed more interested than concerned which surprised Jeff.

"Apparently, your granddad was extremely drunk and took a tumble down the stairs. During the investigation they found deep scratches on the wall where he had tried to stop himself from falling. There were more found on the floor beside his body as if he tried getting up after falling. Determined old bastard. Could have been what

Joshua Marsella

forensics experts call cadaveric spasms I suppose because the papers claimed he died instantly from the fall."

He continued "The whole thing sounded fishy to me, but that's just conspiratorial Jeff talking. Still, I'm not sure why they'd need to lie about it if it was just an accident." He paused and contemplated for a moment, then started again. "Are you *sure* I should even be telling you this? Maybe there's a reason why your mum didn't want you to know." Jeff looked around nervously like he had maybe said too much.

"Please don't tell her I told you. I'm sure it was probably confidential or something. It doesn't pay much but I really need this job. I'm sure my boss wouldn't like to hear I'd been eavesdropping in on his conversations either." His guilty conscience seemed to force him to start sweating profusely.

"No no, it's fine really! My lips are sealed." He locked his lips with the imaginary key again. "I won't tell a soul, I swear. I definitely understand why my mother wouldn't tell me about it. That's gotta be the reason why she never goes down there. Thank you, Jeff. Boy am I glad I ran into *you* today." Connor was unsure how much he really meant that even though he liked the guy. Now that he knew what happened, he wasn't too sure he felt that much better about the situation or the fact that his grandfather died in the house. How could his mother let him move his room down there knowing what had taken place? She must have known the truth would eventually come out.

"Again, sorry for your loss, kid. I know he was your grandpa even if he was a mean guy, but hey, nobody is perfect. On the bright side, at least you guys scored a house out of the deal! A brilliant philosopher once said 'Every silver lining's got a touch of grey.' Okay, it was Jerry Garcia in 1987. One of the great philosophers of my generation. But it's true!"

Connor chuckled. "Thanks Jeff, but like I said, I never met the guy." He thought of the tall dark figure then wondered how true that really was. Was it his grandfather standing behind the curtain, his rank noisome breath finding its way into his nostrils in the dead of night? A shiver ran down his spine. He decided it was time to change the subject and get down to business. "So, how about that Spider-Man!"

"Follow me, good sir!" Jeff finally stood up from his stool and waved his big paw in a 'this way' gesture. "We have an excellent clearance sale going on right now. I'll give you the hookup since we are now friends and all." He flashed Connor another toothy smile but added a playful wink this time.

Connor really did like this guy regardless of the recent grisly and potentially confidential information he had just shared with him about his grandfather. Some truths are better left a mystery. A hard lesson learned.

- Ten -

On his bike ride home from the comic book shop
Connor decided to make a pit stop at the cemetery.
Thomas Hill was the oldest cemetery in town with a few
headstones dating back to the late 19th century. Those
could be found in the back, were old and decrepit with
indecipherable engravings, fringed with moss. The front
half were the more recent additions.

He pedaled toward the back of the lot reading the
random names taking note of the dates as he slowly
coasted by. He was always a little bewildered when he saw
a smaller grave that belonged to a baby or child.
Childhood wasn't supposed to end in death. Death was
reserved for old people. The image of a tiny dead baby
lying in a coffin underground flashed into his mind. It
made him feel heartbroken and disillusioned. Their once
soft pink skin smelling of lotion and powder slowly turned
to shades of grey and purple. The worms and beetles
busily ate away at the decaying wooden coffin eager to get
inside for a tasty meal. The world wasn't as black and
white as his young, naive mind had convinced him. It was
more grey and necrotic looking, it was far bleaker and

depressing. Now the image of the worm riddled baby was securely lodged in his brain.

The cemetery lawn was green with lush grass. Some of the high points had started to turn yellow from the scorching July heat that burned up the ground. He turned the front wheel and headed towards the direction of his house. It wasn't his intention to stop at the grave of his grandfather, but nonetheless he found himself applying the brakes. Now that he stood at the gravesite he noticed just how close it was to their house. Uncomfortably close, just over the rusted chain link fence. He swung his leg over the seat then laid his bike on the ground. He carefully set down the paper bag that contained his newly purchased comics on top of the spokes of his bike wheel.

He walked over to the patch of ground in front of the headstone where the pastor and the gravediggers had gathered a few months before for the burial. He read the words engraved on the face of the granite.

George C. Hanscott
Aug. 22, 1935 - Nov. 29, 1997
Served His Country, Rest In Peace

Connor did some quick math in his head. "63 years old. Served his country?" Connor quietly asked himself. "If he was a veteran then why wasn't he buried with the rest of the soldiers at the VA cemetery?" His class in school had visited the veterans cemetery last year for a field trip in history class during a lesson on World War II. It was a beautiful place that seemed to spread out for miles and the grass never turned yellow there. They were told that if a person served in a war they were eligible to be buried in the cemetery and the costs were covered by the VA. Connor wondered if his mom would know or if he even dared to ask her. Something didn't add up.

As he turned to hop back on his bike something caught his eye. He kneeled down to get a closer look. At the bottom of the headstone he saw 4 light scratches gouged into the granite below the word **PEACE** he hadn't noticed at first. He rubbed his fingers across it curiously wondering who would desecrate the headstone of a soldier? He supposed it could have happened accidentally during the burial. Or perhaps an overly careless caretaker bumped into it with a lawnmower.

Then he noticed something that chilled his bones. There were footprints in the soft ground that appeared to walk away from the gravesite in the direction of the house.

He grabbed his comics, hopped back onto his bike to finish the ride home but remained there for a moment. He stared at the final resting place of his grandfather. So many questions swirled aimlessly around in his head but he didn't know if he would ever get answers to them. His mother seemed determined to never speak about her father again, and Connor felt obliged to respect that.

- Eleven -

That night when Janet got home from work she spotted Connor relaxed on the couch engrossed in one of his new comics with a look of boredom. The house was quiet with the television off. She had a paper bag rolled up at the top gripped firmly in her left hand while her purse hung from her right shoulder. She set them on the table then walked into the living room to greet her son.

"Hey dude! What you got there?" Connor looked up to give her a phoney smile. He tilted the book so she could read off the cover. "Captain America?" She read aloud pretending to sound interested in anything besides pouring herself a glass. The first drink of the evening was always the best.

In a dry tone that lacked any enthusiasm he replied, "Yeah. I rode down to Main Street today on my bike to stop at Downton Comics. I took your advice. Picked up something less scary, but it's also *a lot* less interesting." Connor sighed while rapidly flipped through the pages with his thumb to emphasize his disinterest. He sat the comic on his lap to give her his undivided attention.

Joshua Marsella

Janet placed her hands on her hips feeling a sense of parental accomplishment for once. "Well there! Hopefully you'll stop having those silly nightmares." She opened the door to the fridge, removed one of the bottles of *Jim Beam* from the paper bag then set the other bottle on the empty middle shelf. She walked to the cupboard, pulled out a tall glass then opened the freezer. Connor heard the ice cubes tinkle into the glass. He looked miffed as he turned to see her pour a tall drink with just a splash of soda.

"I brought you home a bottle of Dr. Pepper and one of your favorite Hot Pockets for dinner if you're hungry. I'm beat so I don't have the energy to cook tonight. The store was swamped today!"

This was no big revelation to the boy. "Thanks Ma. I'm not super hungry anyway. Oh yeah, thanks again for the comic money. I actually chatted with the clerk down there. He's a pretty cool guy." Connor thought he'd mention to her what he found out about her father, but decided against it at the last minute. She seemed to be in a fairly good mood so he didn't want to spoil it.

"That's cool bud, you're welcome! Hope you don't mind if I use the tele? I want to catch a bit of the news before the wheel comes on."

"S'all yours. I'll be heading downstairs soon. Kind of beat from the bike ride today. It was nice to get some fresh air. I even took a little ride through the cemetery." He decided to take a chance and ask a question anyway since he felt it was somewhat benign. "Hey, if grandpa served in the military, how come he wasn't buried in the VA cemetery with the other dead soldiers?"

Janet stopped halfway into the living room and tipped her head up toward the ceiling in the universal show of annoyance.

"Seriously Connor? I thought we agreed we weren't going to talk about him anymore"

"I know. I'm really sorry, but his burial costs would have been covered and everything. It just seems odd is all." He glanced down at the glass in her hand wondering to himself when she had switched to the hard stuff.

The burn of the whisky was a relief as it hit the back of her throat. The ice rattled in her glass. She winced as she inhaled deeply through her teeth.

"He was dishonorably discharged then was shipped home from Vietnam before the end of his tour. He got into some bad trouble over there. It had to be really bad to be kicked out of a war. I don't know what exactly and frankly

Joshua Marsella

I don't care to know. He never talked about his time in Vietnam. I mean, why would he? I don't know anymore than that." As she felt her anger rising she took another deep haul of the drink almost emptying the glass.

"Does that answer satisfy you Detective Gale? Jesus! I'd think you were writing a paper about him, you've asked me so many questions." This time she finished off her drink.

"Yes, I'm sorry. Not only for asking you all these questions, but for the way he treated you. I know it's hard for you to talk about him." Connor looked down at a picture of Captain America punching a soldier with a swastika on his sleeve and felt mildly ashamed. He genuinely felt bad he brought him up again possibly ruining his mother's evening. He could sense the pain and embarrassment in her face. He should have just left it alone.

"Thank you Connie, but you don't even know half of it. To be honest, I would prefer to keep it that way. I'd rather you just leave it alone. Don't allow him to live in your head. Just let his miserable ass rot in that grave of his. That's all he deserves!"

Connor looked at his watch then decided to change the subject. He pointed to the t.v. "News is starting. I'm going to go heat up that Hot Pocket. I guess I am kind of hungry after all."

As he stood up to head to the kitchen, she stopped him halfway and placed a hand on his shoulder.

"Please don't feel bad Connor, you're just curious. I know I haven't been very open about what my life was like before you were born. Being inquisitive is a good thing, most of the time. It's just that it's a very sensitive subject for me, but still, I shouldn't take it out on you. Don't forget the D.P. It's in the paper bag." Janet leaned over, playfully ruffled his hair then followed him into the kitchen to refill her glass. "You're going to need a trim soon you little hippy."

Once her glass was full again she reclined in the chair which let out a miserable metallic squeal. The sound of the *Channel 6 News* put an abrupt end to the silence.

Joshua Marsella

- Twelve -

He finished his pepperoni and cheese Hot Pocket at the kitchen table, said goodnight to his mother then walked down to his room to read one more comic book before he hit the hay. This time it was *Spider-Man vs Doc Ock*. He still preferred his *Tales from the Crypt*, but agreed with his mom that those comics may have contributed to his nightmares if that's what they really were. But something inside him knew they weren't totally to blame. Something *was* going on in the house, though he wasn't entirely sure he wanted to figure out what it was. Afterall, it was curiosity that killed the cat.

He decided to sleep with his radio off. His bed had never felt so comfortable. The bike ride and fresh air had tuckered him out making the sleep come quickly.

Out of the darkest corner of the basement, a figure slowly emerged to spy on the sleeping adolescent through a tear in the sheet. The gradual rise and fall of the boy's hairless chest aroused the trespassing onlooker. A gnarled hand began to dig at the wooden house post with long, broken fingernails.

It wasn't long before Connor awoke with that familiar uneasy feeling. He opened his eyes to see nothing except the blackness of the basement. He flipped over in bed. As he was getting ready to readjust his body a familiar stench struck him. This time it was more invasive as if the source was directly in front of him; the combined smells of old booze, wet earth, and decomposition. As he came to he heard the scratches.

SCRAAAAATCH SCRAAAAATCH

He looked out toward the sheets then audibly gasped as he saw the silhouette of the tall dark figure illuminated by the pale glow of the nightlight.

At first he was frozen where he lay in a state of terror. His survival instincts kicked in as he pulled his blankets up to his chin then closed his eyes. He hoped it would magically go away or he would wake up from this nightmare.

"It's only a dream. It's only a dream." he whispered to himself.

After he opened them to still see the brooding figure, he knew he wasn't dreaming. Now wide awake he snapped out of his immobile state to make his move. He needed

Joshua Marsella

answers. This was the real world, not one of his horror movies.

"Hello?" Connor said in a low sort of whimper. No answer. "Hello? Is there someone there? This isn't funny anymore." Still no response. Although he didn't want to move, he quietly kicked off the covers. It was time to see for himself if this was all just a figment of his imagination.

He planted his bare feet on the cold floor. *What in the world am I doing?* He thought to himself as he lowered himself onto his hands and knees. Slowly, he crawled on all fours toward the sheets then peaked underneath where the figure was standing. There was nothing. No feet. No legs.

He peered up but could still see the figure behind the sheet, only now he heard heavy gargled breathing.

Connor almost choked on his inhale when below the sheet a large bare foot dropped to the floor from seemingly out of thin air. As a second foot followed a small quantity of debris cascaded from above and gathered around the feet. It looked like dirt.

"What the hell?" He quietly trembled under his breath.

The figure stood so close that its deep heavy breathing moved the sheet in and out. As he sensed the danger he was in, Connor lifted himself up then fell backwards onto his hands scuffing his soft palms on the concrete. His heart rate accelerated as he let out another deep gasp. He quickly moved backwards in a crab walk fashion until his shoulders bumped into his bed while his eyes never moved off the figure for one second. He felt his way up onto the edge of the mattress, reached for the lamp and turned the knob. Nothing happened. A few more turns still the darkness resisted the light as the lamp remained off.

Not knowing what to do next, he hopped back up onto his bed yanking the blanket up high enough to cover everything but his eyes. He still didn't dare take his eyes off the figure. The shadow started to reach in causing the sheet to gently sway. The outline of a huge dark hand reached in, gripped the edge of the sheet and started to pull open the gap. The heavy breathing stopped to let out a soggy almost mournful moan.

"WHHHHHUUUUU-!"

Connor closed his eyes then let out a blood curdling scream of horror that sounded almost feminine.

"AAAAAAHHHH! *MOOOOOOOM!*"

He kept his eyes sealed shut as his heart pounded in his chest. After a brief moment, he could hear the cadence of running feet above his head. A door opened as Janet reached the top of the stairs. She slapped the switch to the overhead lights to turn them on.

"*Connor! Jesus!* What's going on? Are you okay?" she yelled down the stairwell in a state of exhausted confusion. She'd never heard her son scream like that before and was almost as scared as he was.

Connor hesitantly pulled the blanket down away from his face and opened one eye. The figure was no longer there, the bad odor seemed to follow and the moaning had stopped. The air was back to the old basement smell which he happily welcomed. *What is going on?* he thought to himself.

"*Connor!* Answer me *right* now!" Janet yelled down never descending the stairs. Her words were slurred and her mouth tasted like sludge from a whiskey barrel.

"Mom! I saw it again! I could see it breathing! I saw its feet! It tried coming into my room this time! I wasn't dreaming!" The desperation was evident in his voice.

"Saw what? What are you going on about?" Janet barked in a harsh, irritated tone.

"The person I told you about last time! I actually saw a hand this time and it was breathing Mom! At first it had no feet but then I saw them!" Connor sounded panicked but still resisted leaving his bed. He still didn't feel safe.

"Oh Christ. Not *this* again!" She sounded fully annoyed this time. "There's *nothing* down there, Connor. You were having another nightmare. I shouldn't have let you have the Doctor Pepper before bed. It's *my* fault. The sugar probably got you all wired up." Her head throbbed like a bass drum each time she yelled.

Connor could feel his frustration grow like a tumor. Why would he make something like this up? His mother's refusal to believe him made him boil.

"*MOM!* I was not sleeping! I know what I saw. Why won't you believe me! I could smell it too. It smelled like a pile of dead leaves and roadkill. There's still dirt on the floor! Come see! I think it was trying to get to me." His fear changed to despair as he was on the verge of tears. "My lamp is blown too. I was trapped down here in the dark. Alone."

He reached over to try his lamp again turning the plastic knob. This time the light turned on. Connor let out a low sigh of relief. Part of him was thankful for the light. The other part of him knew it made him look like a liar. "Hm. Well it wouldn't turn on a few minutes ago! I *swear!*"

Joshua Marsella

"Connor, really? You *know* I have to get up early for work. Why are you playing this game? I was worried this would happen if you moved your room down there." She combed her hair out of her face with her splayed fingers.

Connor winced at this. He didn't want his mom to think of him as a scared little kid. He just didn't know how to convince her that what he saw was real. Maybe she didn't want to believe it was real. Maybe she was just as scared. Maybe she couldn't see it even if she did believe. He had never felt so alone or helpless.

"Why don't you grab your pillow and blanket and come sleep on the couch tonight? Tomorrow after work we will discuss the possibility of moving your room back up here. Maybe it won't be so bad if we can find you a fan or something. I need my sleep, kiddo."

Connor felt betrayed and defeated. "Fine, Mom." He grabbed his pillow and blanket. "I'll be up in a minute." Under his breath he mumbled, "It wasn't the damn Doctor Pepper!"

Without even bothering to turn off his lamp he walked towards the stairwell. He reached out to open the sheet but his hand stopped halfway. His eyes widened and his breathing had stopped short of his next breath. He saw a dirty handprint on the edge of the sheet where the thing had grabbed it. He leaned forward, put his nose up close to the print and sniffed. He cringed, then gagged as his nostrils were infiltrated with the awful scent of decay and something worse. He didn't know how he knew, but he was positive the smell was death.

- Thirteen -

The next morning Connor could sense that something was seriously wrong with the house they now called home. He decided if his mother was going to ignore the problem and pretend it didn't exist that he would have to figure it out by himself. The only problem was he had no idea where to start or what he was looking for. Most of the house was cleared out before they moved in. Much of it was donated to local charity and the rest was sold or brought to a landfill. The only original stuff that remained was some of the furniture, all the appliances, and a few boxes of junk that remained in the basement. He didn't have much to go by.

After Janet left in the morning for the early shift, he thought it would be a good time to do a little detective work. He needed answers that wouldn't come to him by conventional means. He scoured the main floor but came up dry since they had disposed of the few remnants of his grandfather's existence. At least the stuff that served them no purpose. Next came the basement. This too had essentially been emptied out so there wasn't much to look through. Janet had made sure that most of her father's personal belongings were removed from the house before they moved in. She made her best effort to make sure no memory of him remained in the house.

As Connor ascended the basement stairs feeling defeated, a memory flashed in his mind. He recalled seeing a small door in the ceiling tucked away in his mother's closet when he helped her hang up her clothes during the move.

Of course! The attic. This was the quintessential place you went when you needed to hide something of importance. Everyone universally hated going up into attics. If there was nothing up there, there was likely nothing in this house. The question remained; what exactly had he expected to find up there in the dark?

He felt guilty as he snooped around in there. He opened her closet and spotted the opening in the ceiling that was lined with trim. A piece of plywood laid across the inside that was painted to match the ceiling. *Bingo.* Now he needed to find a way to get up there.

At first he thought he could stand on one of the kitchen chairs, but after one unsuccessful attempt he found that he was too short to reach the hole.

Then he remembered seeing a short, rusty extension ladder leaned against the back of the house one day when he put his bike away. Once he replaced the chair he walked around to the back yard. He picked up the ladder and shook off the morning dew that accumulated on it. Carefully he carried it inside trying not to bang up the walls.

At first he struggled to lift it into the closet, but after a few grunts and groans he managed to extend it up, set it against the inside of the hole then steadied the base. He ran into the kitchen to pull a green military issue flashlight out of the junk drawer. One of those remnants of George that remained behind only because they found it useful. He flipped the switch to make sure it worked. He returned to the closet then carefully climbed the aluminum ladder.

When he reached the top his nerves kicked in. He became unsure of what he was doing or why he was doing it. His mental gymnastics weren't enough to make him back down. He closed his eyes, inhaled a deep breath to calm his nerves and reassure himself. Like most people, attics creeped him out. He slowly lifted up on the piece of wood with one hand holding onto the ladder with the other. He half expected a dead body to fall out of the hole upon opening but no such thing happened. The plywood was surprisingly lightweight. A gust of stale heat and clumps of dust hit him in the face as he climbed. He swatted at his face in an instant panic imagining it was spiders raining down on him. After he cleared three more rungs on the ladder he hoisted the upper half of his body into the attic. He clicked on the flashlight while still balanced on the ladder to have a look around inside.

He was surprised by how dark the attic was in the middle of the day. The flashlight beam illuminated roof trusses and a few blotches of what appeared to be black mold in all directions. Looking down at the top side of the ceiling he noticed more insulation with dark brown oval-shaped pellets scattered along the top. Mouse poop. That could potentially explain away the scratching noises he had heard, except he hadn't come across any of the fecal matter in the basement. He also noticed rough cut wooden planks that formed a sort of walkway laying across the horizontal joists.

At the far end of the attic where the light would barely reach, the planks ended. He could just make out a dark green box with a small bronze padlock on it that shimmered as the light hit it.

He was careful not to touch the insulation or tiny feces as he worked his way onto the planks. He kept his head ducked down as he cautiously walked across the boards with his free hand while reaching up and holding onto the roof trusses overhead in a monkey bar fashion.

Sweat started to accumulate on his forehead almost immediately. His body slightly quivered at the sight of a tiny skeleton that formerly belonged to a mouse. He wondered what had happened to the guts and fur that used to make up the critter's body. Did it just decompose or were mice cannibalistic? Skeletons in real life were much creepier than in his comics. Even mouse skeletons.

He decided to just focus on his task. After a couple more cautious steps he was standing directly in front of the wide foot locker. It was sitting on a piece of particle board plywood pushed up against the wall. This was about as well-hidden as anything could be in a small house like this.

Much to his surprise, the padlock was unsecured but still hung from the latch of the foot locker. He inspected the top of the container then noticed faded lettering stenciled onto the face of the lid under a thin thin layer of dust. He focused the light onto the words, wiped the dust with his hand and read:

USMC - SERGEANT GEORGE C. HANSCOTT
US5563891-C
C CO 3RD PLATOON
DA NANG AIR BASE, VIETNAM

He removed the padlock then lifted the top part of the brass latch. Unsure what to expect he held his breath in anticipation, lifted the lid with care then tipped it back against the wall. He wasn't surprised by what he found, not at first.

On the left side of the container there was a green folder with the words '*DISCHARGE FORMS*' stamped on the front that was filled with paperwork. This was stacked on top of other folders filled with orders and military jargon that didn't interest him since he knew he wouldn't understand a majority of it.

On the right side he saw an old pair of dusty black combat boots neatly stacked on top of some folded clothing. He picked up the boots and heard a metallic jingling as something fell out of one of them. He picked up a set of dog tags that hung from a metal beaded chain. One metal tag was stamped with his grandfather's name, his social security number, the letters O Pos, and METHODIST. This hung from the longer chain while a second tag hung on a smaller chain dangling from the first. Although he was mildly interested, he tossed these onto the pile of paperwork.

With both hands he gently lifted out the worn green uniform which he saw had two patches sewn onto each shoulder of the jacket. He was sure these carried some significance, but they meant nothing to him. Underneath was a pair of matching pants. He set these both aside then he finally found something he thought could be of interest.

An old beat up shoebox was sitting in the bottom corner of the foot locker. It had ***Hanoi*** written on the lid in bold black marker. Below the words was a small hand drawn smiley face. This piqued his curiosity.

He lifted the box out of the container and started to remove the cardboard lid. Before he could do so, a quiet scratching noise broke the silence behind him in the darkness. Startled, he snapped his head around followed by the beam of the flashlight only to see a shiny pair of tiny beady eyes stare back at him from the corner of the attic.

The mouse squeaked then scurried down into the insulation.

Daylight was pouring up from his mother's closet through the opening in the ceiling. He suddenly felt very claustrophobic in the dark, humid attic. He picked up the shoebox and tightly tucked it under his arm like a tailback, being careful not to spill its unknown contents. He felt slightly disappointed by what he had found since nothing appeared to be revealing. He hoped he had found something worthy of his investigation inside the shoebox. He used his other hand to hang on as he made his way back to the ladder a bit more swiftly.

Connor descended the ladder with the shoebox. He meticulously cleaned up the evidence of his investigation then vacuumed the fallen debris. He didn't want his mother to know he had gone into the attic before he knew if he had actually found anything. She wouldn't have appreciated him creeping around her room no matter what the reason and she certainly wouldn't have allowed him into the attic. It would have to remain a secret between him and the mouse that had spied on him.

Joshua Marsella

- Fourteen -

Connor had no idea what to expect when he opened the shoebox. He didn't even know what Hanoi was except that it was most likely a place in Vietnam. He walked to the kitchen then set the box down on the table. Quietly he sat there for a couple of minutes with his hands on the sides of the box. He spun it around inspecting all the sides as an attempt to delay what was inevitable. So far he had determined that this was the box the combat boots were issued in.

Trying not to get his hopes up, he finally gathered up the courage to remove the lid.

Inside he found a small bundle wrapped in a rag. He picked it up, then started to unravel what turned out to be a t-shirt. What he found inside shook him to his core almost immediately robbing the boy of whatever sliver of childhood innocence he still hung on to.

His investigation came to a grinding halt as he ran to the bathroom to throw up his breakfast. At that moment he wanted nothing more than for his mom to come home and he wanted to be out of that house. Mostly he wished he'd never gone up into the attic or opened that damn box.

He walked to the couch then turned on the television to watch some lighthearted sitcoms until his mother came home from work. He needed something to take his mind off what he'd seen.

* * *

A good part of the day passed by before Janet drove into the driveway. She felt burnt out from her busy shift and was overcome with a sense of dread when she thought about having to cook dinner. Perhaps it would be a good night to have a pizza delivered. Connor would love that. A real pizza. Not just a frozen hot pocket nuked in the microwave.

She'd been kind of hard on him lately but she knew it was for his own good. She didn't understand why he was so curious about her father and she didn't like the constant interrogations. She also knew that George was technically the only family besides her that he ever heard anything about. That's because there was no other family.

Her only hope was that her son would make some friends in the fall once school started. That would help take his mind off the unpleasantries. Janet grabbed her purse then headed up to the house fully oblivious to the fact that it would be her last time doing so.

Connor had unintentionally dozed off on the couch during an episode of *Who's the Boss?* He awoke when his mother shut her car door.

"Oh come on! Cut-it-out!" Uncle Joey joked to Danny Tanner pretending his fingers were scissors. *Full House* was on the television which meant it was going to be dinner time soon. The thought made Connor's stomach growl like a hungry wolf eyeing a juicy rabbit.

He rubbed his balled fists into his eyes and yawned. For a moment he had almost forgotten about what unfolded earlier. What he'd found in the attic. Unfortunately his blissful ignorance was short lived. It all quickly rushed back to him forcing him to sit up in a panic once he realized he had left the opened shoebox on the table.

The kitchen door swung open as Janet walked into the house. Tired from her long day at the store and more than ready for a drink. He was too late to avoid what happened next.

"Hey buddy!" Her voice was surprisingly cheerful. "What's goin-" Her question was cut short by what she saw spread out in front of her. Before she even had time to set her purse down she found the contents of the shoebox on the table.

It was a collection of old polaroids. Most of the pictures were stacked up face down but the ones Connor had seen were scattered when he had fled to the bathroom.

"What the fuck am I looking at Connor?" The purse dropped to the floor. He always knew when she was truly angry because she would curse without excusing her French.

"Mom, I have-" she didn't give him the opportunity to finish before cutting him off mid-sentence.

"What are these? Where did you get them? You better start talking!" Her voice kept getting louder as her tone got harsher with each word.

"I-I found them. In the a-attic. In a-a foot locker that belonged to grandpa." He cowered then joined her at the table. Shame for what he had done was written all over his face and his nerves caused him to stutter.

"Jesus H. Christ! What in God's name were you doing in the attic?" She picked up a handful of the photographs and started shuffling through them. She kept covering her mouth with the back of her hand like she was fighting the urge to vomit. "What were you doing up there, Connor?" she asked almost in tears. "*Answer me!*"

"I'm s-sorry Mom! I told you some weird stuff had been h-happening to me in the basement but you wouldn't believe me!" he answered, fighting back his own tears.

He had never seen his mother cry before so it hurt him to see her this way. Even more so knowing he was responsible.

Janet lifted one of the polaroids up close to take a closer look. She could see a small room in what appeared to be a bamboo hut. There were two people lying on the floor. Bodies. One was a woman with a bullet hole in the middle of her forehead. Blood oozed into her eyes that were wide open staring straight ahead as if looking into the camera. The other was a man that had a deep gash across his throat. His white tank top was saturated in dark, syrupy blood. His eyes were mercifully closed. They were leaned up against each other in the corner of the room on the floor as if they had been tossed there like dirty laundry. A young soldier was knelt down beside them. He wore a wide grin on his clean shaven face giving the photographer a thumbs up like he was posing with a prize deer.

"Christ on a fucking stick! That's my father. That's George!" She dropped the picture on the table then hesitantly flipped to another polaroid with an anguished look on her face.

The next photo caused a sudden rush of nausea to well up in her stomach. Her father appeared to be focused as he sawed the ear off the dead man with a bayonet, still wearing the same sickly grin. He was clearly enjoying himself. His face showed no remorse. Just when she thought she'd seen the worst of it, the photos got darker and more disturbing.

That was when Connor walked over to the counter and started fixing his mother a drink; the same whiskey on ice that she had the night before. As inappropriate as he realized it was, he knew she would need something to numb the pain of what she was about to see.

The next picture involved young George pulling a young tearful girl out from under a bed by her skinny arm. An arm not much bigger than Connor's own.

The next one showed George sitting with his arm around her waist on the bed not far from her dead parents.

He was flashing another thumbs up at the camera still wearing that vile grin.

Janet was in no way prepared for what came next.

Connor handed his mom the chilled glass of whiskey as she picked up the last few polaroids seemingly against her will. She didn't want to see anymore, but something inside her wouldn't let her stop. She sipped off the glass without acknowledging her son.

The last few pictures involved George cutting the young girl's clothing off with the same bloodied blade he'd murdered her father with. The girl looked to be sobbing but too small and weak to fight off the sturdy young marine. The last photo she saw involved her father climbing on top of the girl pinning her to the bed where her parents had slept soundly the night before. He looked to be unbuckling his belt. That was it. She'd seen more than enough.

Janet's face turned deathly pale before she simultaneously dropped the pictures and the glass. The glass shattered on the floor. The photographs dropped into the puddle of whiskey, ice cubes and broken glass. Forcibly shoving her hand to her mouth to avoid throwing up on the floor she turned, half running, half staggering then ripped open the porch door which clattered against the wall.

As his mother lost her lunch over the porch railing, Connor gathered up the whiskey dampened polaroids with the ones that were strewn out on the table then wrapped them back up in the t-shirt. He didn't want to see them ever again. He inconspicuously slid something into his back pocket then shoved the bundle back into the box; though not before he noticed the remainder of the box's contents he'd missed before.

In the box beside the bundle sat a long tin pencil case. He looked out at his mom just as she spat over the railing then wiped her mouth before dry heaving one more time.

He reached in then quietly cracked open the case. Immediately, he dropped the case like he'd been bitten by a snake. The contents spilled out into the shoebox. They were ears. Putrefied human ears that had been severed then strung together with a long piece of twine. George's trophy necklace.

Connor grabbed the lid and slammed it down on the shoebox. He didn't need to see anymore to know his grandfather was even worse than he could have ever imagined. He was a murderer. A rapist. A real life monster.

Everything suddenly made perfect sense as to why his mother hated the man so much. She'd clearly seen him for what he really was even before she saw his macabre collection.

Janet walked back into the kitchen then straight to the sink. She cupped her hand under the running faucet raising the cool water to her mouth rinsing out the lingering taste of bile and whiskey. She spat a few times then stood there, leaned over the sink attempting to slow her breathing. Perspiration had beaded on her forehead as she was shaking uncontrollably.

"Mom. I-I am really, *really* sorry for going up in the attic. I would have never gone snooping around if I had any idea-" She turned raising her left hand to signal him to stop talking. Then she pointed to a chair.

"Please sit down, Connor. We need to have a talk." She had regained some of the peach color back in her complexion but was still visibly shaken. "There's something I need to discuss with you and it's not going to be easy, so please just let me talk. I may have some answers to your questions."

Janet fixed herself a much needed new drink before she sat down in the chair next to Connor. She lifted the glass to her lipstick smeared lips and took a long swig of her whiskey.

"As you know I had a rough childhood. I've told you many times about how my father was abusive and that he would get drunk then take out his aggressions on my mother and I, but mostly just me. My mother would fight back but she would pay the price for it. I was too small and helpless. Well... it wasn't just the physical and verbal abuse." She inhaled deeply, then exhaled through puckered lips. Connor could smell her sour breath.

"He used to go out after dinner drinking at the bar until late into the evening. Eventually, long after my mom and I had gone to bed, he would stumble back into the house completely shitfaced. I could sometimes hear him talking to himself, but it sounded as though he thought someone was with him. Like he was having a conversation." She took another drink.

"Remember, I was just a little girl at the time. Younger than you are now. I had no idea what was going on with him. It happened so regularly that it seemed perfectly normal. Just Dad being Dad. Sometimes he'd push open my bedroom door and just stand there watching me sleep. I wasn't really asleep but I would pretend to be because I knew it was way past my bedtime. He scared me and I didn't want to make him mad. He had a habit of scratching his long fingernails on my door jamb. He hated trimming his nails. Well, at one point he actually started coming into my room then would sit on the edge of my bed in nothing but his underwear because that's how he liked to sleep." She shifted in her chair looking uncomfortable, then broke eye contact with her son.

"Then- eventually, he started to lay down in my bed beside me. He'd crawl under the covers like it was completely natural. My bed was too small for two people so I would be trapped between him and the wall. I was so little. He seemed so massive." Tears started to well up in her eyes and her lips were quivering.

"I could smell the sour stench of booze on his breath he was breathing so heavily. It was nauseating. At times I tried to hold my breath but I was afraid he would notice. At first he would just cuddle with me, but I felt him looking me up and down. Then he started doing worse things to me. Touching me in places I knew he shouldn't have been and making awful moaning noises. There was nothing I could do to stop him! I just kept my eyes shut tight and tried to imagine I was somewhere else."

The pitch of her voice was so high, it was almost childlike. Connor was too embarrassed to look up at her, so he just sat as stiff as a statue and stared down at his small hands. He'd never heard his mother talk like this before and he didn't like it. Her childhood was much worse than he ever could have imagined. What the hell did he have to complain about?

"Well, after things continued to escalate he would stop me in the hallway as I walked by him. He'd grab me hard by the shoulder and he'd grin at me like he was being playful, but I knew he wasn't. He would whisper threats at me through gritted teeth. Warning me that if I ever told my mom about the things he was doing that he'd hurt her or even kill her if *I* made him. Said he would chain us up down in the basement, scratch out our eyeballs then starve us in the darkness until we were dead. And it would be all my fault. Made me promise to keep it a secret. I had no choice. I didn't want him to hurt my mother!"

Connor now appreciated her rational fear of the basement. The thought of being chained up as a prisoner and left to die down there chilled him to the bone.

"Well, this happened off and on for several years until I was a couple years older than you. Probably 14 or so. My mom was never very attentive, but she started acting suspicious when I asked her to take me to the doctor one day. I was worried because my period was late, but of course I didn't really know what was going on."

Connor started to feel uncomfortable with the conversation and he too shifted in his seat. He didn't know what that meant as she'd never given him *the talk*, but he still remained silent. He wouldn't know what to say even if she hadn't told him not to interrupt, nor did this seem like the appropriate time to inquire about the mysteries of the female anatomy.

She continued, "I noticed my mom got real distant towards me and was fighting with my father a lot more than usual. She had caught on to the fact that he had occasionally slept in my room after coming home drunk, but she could never have imagined what was going on. She needed answers so she called my doctor to get them. Well, her suspicions were confirmed. Her daughter who had never had a boyfriend before was now somehow pregnant. After she got off the phone with the doctor she wouldn't talk to me or even look at me."

"When my father got home from work that day he joined her in their bedroom. They had a bad fight but my mother dominated the conversation. Even though I knew she was mad at me, I was worried for her safety. I could hear things being thrown around and glass smashing. I was so scared that I just laid down on my bed in the fetal position. I never learned if he admitted to what he was doing because the next thing I knew my mother was packing a suitcase. She left in a taxi cab while he yelled at her on her way out the door begging her to stop. She never said goodbye to me. Never said a word to me." Janet's eyes were bloodshot, tears were streaming down her face.

"Never even looked at me when she left. That was the last time I ever saw or heard from her. She was disgusted with me like it was somehow my fault. Thought I was an abomination. Just walked out never looking back. She didn't want to stay in this house for another minute. Same way I have felt since we got here." The shame and embarrassment was clearly evident on her face.

Connor started to feel sick to his stomach.

"Soon after, I ran away from home. There was no way I would have survived living in this house with that animal. That *monster*! I was a pregnant 15 year old girl with nowhere to go. An outcast. I hitched rides for several months to get away. I fought off predatory perverts that would pick me up hoping to get a piece of ass. Almost died jumping out of a moving car on a couple occasions. I didn't get too far. Was too scared to leave the state. I knew I needed to get to a hospital. That's where I eventually gave birth to a beautiful, perfect baby boy."

"When I turned 18 I legally changed my last name to Gale. As in Dorothy Gale, the girl from my favorite movie as a kid. You know, *The Wizard of Oz*? I didn't want my dad to ever be able to track me down."

Connor didn't want to hear the rest of what she was going to say. He wanted to stand up and run out of the house at that very moment. Pretend like today never happened.

"Do you understand what I'm trying to tell you, Connor?" She put her hand on top of his tightly clenched fists. By now she was sobbing and had a hard time saying the next part. The part that would shatter the previously known understanding of his existence.

He still didn't have the courage to look her in the eyes.

"*You* were that baby. *You* are my only baby. My only child. *My* father George- is also your father. That's why-"

Connor tore his hands away from hers. His face was red with embarrassment but his expression was that of disgust. He stood up, backed away from the table, kicked the chair out from under him and knocked it into the refrigerator. He was violently shaking his head trying to unhear what he just heard.

"NO! YOU LIE! THAT'S NOT TRUE! YOU SAID MY DAD LEFT US BEFORE I WAS A BORN! YOU'RE A LIAR! A LIAAAAR!" He could feel the rage build up inside but his head felt dizzy.

He wanted to leave that house. In that kitchen with his mother was the absolute last place he wanted to be. As he ran through the open kitchen door Janet attempted to reach out to grab him but missed. He jumped off the porch as she yelled his name while she ran after him outside. The scene reminded her of the last time she saw her mother.

"Connor! Please come back!" He heard the anguish and desperation in her voice even in his haste to get away, but his searing anger wouldn't let him turn around.

He hopped onto his bike mid stride and pedaled away as fast as his legs could operate. He had nowhere to go, but he was going there fast. His mind swirled in a state of turbulence so he didn't look before he turned onto

Joshua Marsella

Thomas Hill Road. Part of him had hoped a car might run him over putting an end to the shame and misery that he was feeling. He had no such luck.

- Fifteen -

As the hot summer day slowly turned to dusk, Connor started to make his way back home. To the house that was built by the monster. The monster that was his father.

His mind still raced, reaching for answers that wouldn't come. Part of him knew he already had all the answers, but he didn't want to believe the truth. Denial was a hell of a drug. Maybe that was how his mother felt when he tried to convince her of what was going on in the basement. Sometimes the truth was darker than one's perceived reality. Ignorance really could be blissful.

He didn't know what to expect when he got home. As it was, he felt horrible for having called her a liar then running out on her at a time when she was the most vulnerable he'd ever seen. He knew what happened to her wasn't her fault, but he was so perturbed he didn't know what else to do.

That evening seemed to drag on for eternity. While he biked around aimlessly for hours, he couldn't help but wonder how his mother held onto that secret for such a long time. That painful truth must have been eating away at her like cancer.

Suddenly everything made so much sense. Her inability to handle a relationship. Her struggles with employment. The sudden bout of alcoholism as soon as they moved into her childhood home. What he had passed off as bad parenting for so long was actually a woman who was suffering from a serious trauma. A trauma that she was reminded of every time she looked at her son. Every time she walked into the house they inherited. This realization hit him hard and he was stricken with guilt. He had to apologize to her. In truth, he was all she had.

The worst day of his life was now behind him. The waxing crescent moon reigned supreme. The solace of the streetlights as the darkness approached did little to ease his loneliness. He hadn't seen a car drive by for quite some time.

His tires skidded to a halt as he reached the end of their driveway. The lamp in the living room was the only light he could see. The porch was dark and uninviting, lit only by the dim moonlight. He opted to get off the bike to walk it up the dirt driveway to the house. As he did so, he stared into the front window trying to catch a glimpse of his mother but did not see her anywhere.

He leaned his bike against the wooden post under the porch, proceeded to walk up the steps, then finally approached the door. In the darkness he felt like a burglar skulking up to the home of his next mark. The minute distance felt like a mile.

He walked into the kitchen and noticed there were no dishes in the sink. It appeared she hadn't eaten dinner. The only smell he could make out was the unmistakable fermented scent of the whiskey puddle that had begun to dry up on the floor among the shards of broken glass. The ice had long since melted. The shoebox no longer sat on the table where he had left it. He wondered if she had found the trophy necklace.

Relief swept over him with the thought that she had thrown the box in the trash, but that was too risky. There would be all sorts of trouble if a garbage man or someone else found the box of pictures and the ears of George's victims in the rubbish. Fire was the only option. The box needed to be burned. His hope was that with the burning of the box that carried the relics of his father's evil deeds, the dark entity that haunted him would be abolished, cleansing the house. Maybe it would grant his mother a peace that she had never known. His mind was made up, but the ceremony would have to wait until dawn.

Connor continued onto the living room. The house felt abandoned and the air was unfamiliar as if someone else lived there. An episode of *M*A*S*H* was on the television but the laugh track seemed out of place with no audience to watch. He knew his mother despised that sitcom, so why would she pick this show to watch tonight of all nights? Things weren't adding up.

There were two empty bottles of Jack Daniels sitting on the coffee table which was not her usual spot to veg out in the evenings. Also, it wouldn't be possible for her to finish off two full bottles of hard stuff in a single night.

"Jesus-" Connor softly spoke aloud. "Is she trying to kill herself?" His head shook in disbelief. He walked over to the television and turned it off as the show's end credits scrolled by.

Now the house was dead silent. No sign of his mother anywhere. He checked the bathroom. No Janet. He quietly walked down the dark hallway to her bedroom and placed his ear on the door. He could hear her snoring so he turned the knob with the utmost care so he wouldn't wake her. He pushed it open just a crack to peek in and check on her. Her room smelled bitter like a distillery floor. He felt relieved knowing she was safe in her bed, but was quickly overwhelmed with grief.

Reminded of the awful things he had said to her earlier that day, he felt a wave of sorrow wash over him. This woman wasn't perfect by any means. She had flaws like every person does. Even so, she worked her butt off everyday at a cruddy gas station to make sure he had enough food on the table, a roof over his head, and the occasional comic book money. She worked through all her problems she dealt with internally but she never complained about it. She was robbed of a normal childhood by her father who repeatedly abused her for his own sadistic pleasures. Abandoned by her mother who was repulsed by her for something she had no control over.

No, she wasn't perfect but she did her best to provide her son with a decent childhood that she herself was deprived of. She allowed him to be himself. A socially awkward kid who didn't have many friends and loved to read horror comics. Let him listen to any music he chose. Let him ride his bike to town. He was lucky to have such a laid back mother. More importantly, she loved him. But like her mother, he abandoned her in her time of need. Her only son. Her only living blood relative.

Yes, he felt like the biggest piece of shit as he stood in the hallway and listened to his mother sleep.

Now who was the monster? As they say, the apple doesn't fall far from the tree.

Connor snuck into the room and rounded the bed. He pulled up the tangled blankets to cover his mother and gently brushed her hair out of her face with his index finger. He stood there for a moment watching her sleep in the darkness. She looked so innocent and peaceful.

That was the first moment he'd ever considered how lucky he was to have her in his life. He leaned over and kissed her softly on the forehead, tip-toed out of her room then quietly closed the door. *God, what is that awful smell in there?* he wondered to himself.

A tall figure hunkered down in the dark corner of the bedroom. It stood there silently garbed only in dirty underwear as it watched the whole sentimental episode. Its heavy breathing was almost lustful as it stared cravingly at the sleeping woman on the bed.

Connor returned to the kitchen to finish cleaning up the spilled whiskey and broken glass. Before heading to bed he stopped at the bathroom to relieve himself and brush his teeth. He paused before he descended the stairs to his bedroom for what would be, unbeknownst to him, the final time. He gazed down at the floor where his father had met his grisly fate. He reached over and fingered the deep scratches in the plaster that ran partway down the wall. The failed attempt of an old man trying to delay his inevitable oncoming death. *What was going through his mind as he fell?* He thought to himself. *Was he scared? Did he even know what was happening?*

Unsure of why he was so curious knowing now what he knew, he tried to shake the image from his mind. The last thing he needed tonight was more gruesome imagery in his head.

Connor walked down the steep stairs while he tried not to imagine what it would be like to stumble and plunge headfirst against his will. His eyes locked onto the patch of carpet at the foot of the steps.

When he reached the bottom he sidestepped off onto the cement floor avoiding the carpet altogether. He bent down and lifted the patch up. This exposed dark stains and more deep scratches similar to those on the wall above. *Jeff was right.* He thought as a chill passed through his body. He dropped the loose piece of carpet and backed away clumsily almost tripping over his own feet.

Burnt out from the craziness of the day and the hours of bike pedaling, he retreated to his room. He thought he'd do a little reading before he passed out for the night.

After rereading the *Spider-Man* comic he pulled out his hidden copy of *Creepshow* from under the mattress. The cartoon stories now felt amatuer and almost comical compared to what he'd experienced earlier that day.

Halfway through the opening story his stomach growled to remind him that he hadn't eaten dinner. He tossed the beat up comic onto the foot of his bed and decided to head back upstairs to nuke the last Hot Pocket he had waiting for him in the freezer.

When he reached the hanging sheet wall he was startled by a familiar voice that broke the air of silence.

The Rolling Stones jammed out of his clock radio speakers with Mick Jagger singing *Paint It Black.*

"What the hell?" Connor walked over, switched off the radio then picked up the flashlight he found earlier that day. He continued his approach to the stairs with the nightlight lighting his way.

Just before he set his barefoot onto the bottom step, the radio switched itself back on at full volume. Connor jumped so hard he nearly tripped and fell. He flipped the switch to the overhead lights but they didn't turn on. He stood there in the darkness and tried the switch again without success. The nightlight and his bedroom lamp were his only sources of light so he turned on the flashlight.

Readied for his approach to run up the stairs, he glanced up but was surprised by his mother standing on the top step. Her figure was silhouetted by a dim light that shined down from the hallway. He aimed the beam of light up at her and saw her eyes were closed. She appeared to be heavily sedated.

"M-mom?" No response. It was as though she couldn't hear or see her son as she stood at attention wearing just her nightgown. He moved a foot up one step and the other remained on the carpet. "Hey! Mom, what are you doing? You okay?" The flashlight flickered. Connor tapped the bottom with his palm and it shone bright again.

Janet raised her left hand out to the side and dug her fingernails into the plaster while she took a heavy step down. Her painted fingernails made a loud, almost unbearable scratching sound. Connor felt the stairwell shake as her foot dropped.

"Mom! Wake up! You need to get back to bed. You're going to fall!"

The *Stones* continued to rock out at full blast in the background. The song sounded heavily distorted blasting out of the small alarm clock speakers.

Janet took another heavy step down towards her son. Her long nails left deep gouges in the wall and plaster debris spilled down onto the stairs. Connor wanted to cover his ears but he needed his hands at the ready in case his mother fell.

"MO-!" Connor felt a hard lump well up in his throat as he froze in terror. He could see a tall, dark figure standing behind his mother in the hallway a few feet away from her. At first glance he thought it was her enlarged shadow from the flashlight beam until a guttural, choked laugh echoed off the walls of the stairwell sending a chill down his spine.

He watched in terror as a veined, corpse-like hand with grayed boney fingers and long, broken fingernails was placed on Janet's right shoulder. There were gobs of mud built up under the ends of the nails. Connor gulped but couldn't move.

The brooding figure spoke only one word in a deep, boisterous voice.

"CATCH!"

The dead hand thrust forward with great force and pushed Janet's unresponsive body down the stairwell towards her son. As she fell, her arms stretched out to her sides like she was a baby bird attempting its first flight. Her silky nightgown looked angelic while she freefalled down to him as if she was floating underwater. Connor reacted instantly by squaring up his body and putting his scrawny arms up to soften her fall the best he could. Her body felt lifeless as she collided with the young boy with no resistance. He managed to catch his mother but was forced back by the heavy weight of the full grown woman. His back slammed against the wall and the last thing he felt was his skull hitting the stone and mortar foundation. They both collapsed unconscious onto the carpet in a heap of tangled arms and legs.

Only a brief moment had passed, but Janet felt as though she'd been sleeping all night. Her head pulsed in agony as she opened her eyes. Her vision was blurred with drunken vertigo as she looked around bewildered. Unaware of where she was, until she noticed Connor unconscious beneath her on the floor at the bottom of the stairs. Her pulse quickened anxiously as the reality of where she was set in.

The flashlight lay next to him on the concrete flickering on and off. The radio had fallen silent.

"Connor?" She shook her son's shoulder. "Connor, wha-what's going on?" He still didn't respond. She steadied herself up onto her knees then gently placed her hands on either side of his head cupping his ears. His skinny body felt lifeless.

"CONNOR!" Her fingertips on the back of his head felt warm and sticky. She pulled her hand away to see her fingers covered in blood. The sanguine fluid looked dark orange in the yellow glow of the nightlight. "Oh my God, *CONNOR! WAKE UP!*" she yelled with a quiver in her voice while her eyes began to well up with tears which worsened her blurred vision.

A ghoulish laugh echoed down the stairwell toward the pair. Janet lost her breath recognizing the laugh from long ago, but couldn't bring herself to look up to see if this was really happening. It felt like a vivid nightmare. A familiar sense of terror she hadn't felt since she was a small girl hit her like the front end of a buick. She slowly stood up. The abrupt rush of blood to her wobbly legs nearly made her lose her balance and fall over.

Lucky for her an eruption of adrenaline helped her quickly overcome the tingly sensation as her motherly instincts kicked into high gear. This was not the time to let her fears get the better of her. Her son needed her.

"Come on Connie, we need to go! Now!" She shoved her hands underneath her son's armpits and lifted him off the bloodied carpet. She could see a small stream of blood running from the back of his head, down his neck staining his white t-shirt. It reminded her of the photographs of the dead Vietnamese man from earlier now hidden under her bed waiting to be burned. She walked backwards dragging her son on his heels towards the bulkhead door. She knew it was their only escape.

THUD SCRAAATCH THUD SCRAAATCH THUD

Joshua Marsella

The bloated corpse of her father started to descend the stairs one at a time. Several of his mangled fingernails peeled back and hung onto the cadaverous flesh as he scratched at the walls. He only moved as fast as his decaying legs would allow while clumps of cemetery dirt and hungry maggots bounced off the wooden tread with each footfall.

Janet could not panic. She refused to look at the monster she last saw laying on the embalming table at the Burnchester morgue. She only had room for two thoughts in her mind. *Escape* and *survive.*

"Connor, now would be a great time to wake up hunny!" She had no idea if her son was still alive, but talking to him as if he were provided her some much needed comfort. Connor's limp body couldn't have weighed more than 75 pounds, but felt like 200.

As sweat rolled down her chin, they reached the rusty red bulkhead doors. On all fours, she climbed the stairs and felt for the locking bar but it was surprisingly unlocked. She pushed open both doors simultaneously.

The chaos of the last few minutes had forced her into a state of sobriety.

"Mmm-mom?" Connor groaned as he started to regain semi-consciousness. His head felt like it'd been smashed with a sledge hammer.

Their father was nearly at the bottom of the stairs.

THUD   THUD

"CONNOR! You're alright!?" Janet sounded elated as her feet pounded back down the steps. "Oh thank *God*! We need to go buddy. Can you walk?" She placed her hand under his arm for support.

Finally they heard one last muffled *THUD*. George now stood on the patch of blood-soaked carpet which hid the spot where he'd met his demise.

"I think so. My head hurts. What happened?" With no sense of urgency he started to stand up while his mother gently lifted him. His collision with the wall had caused him to forget their situation was dire. Once he was upright Janet bolted back up the stairs to show him the way out.

"*Come on*! You need to hurry!" Janet was finally in panic mode.

The strobe of the flashlight grabbed his attention. It created the illusion of a dance floor giving George's movements an eerie delay effect. In the glow of the nightlight, he caught a glimpse of the monster that haunted him the last few weeks. The monster that had haunted his mother for all of her childhood and her dreams as an adult even in death. The monster he now knew as his father.

Connor felt bewitched by some dark spell. His feet felt as if they were cemented to the floor. His father looked exactly like one of the living dead from one of his horror comics. This wasn't at all how he'd imagine their first rendezvous.

George wore nothing but a pair of underwear that were blotched with dark stains. One of his arms was bent in the wrong direction with a jagged bone protruding from beneath the torn flesh. His eye sockets were hollow and dark. His lips had been eaten away by beetles and maggots that hungrily dined on the soft flesh. This exposed a set of broken black teeth and gums like he was attempting to smile at his son. The same evil grin from the polaroids, but worse. Like something out of a nightmare. This was no movie.

"Come be with me, son." The dead man choked out his final words to his son in a muddy gargled lisp. Half his tongue had been bitten off in the fall. The rancid odor expelled from the corpse's mouth overwhelmed Connor's senses. His empty stomach pushed forth a bit of stinging bile that burned his throat. George stiffly raised his brittle arm and longingly reached a claw out toward the boy.

The dazed boy slowly began to lift his arm as if he welcomed the invitation to finally unite with the father he never knew.

"D-Dad?" The word felt foreign to him.

"CONNOR! NOW!!" Janet shrieked from her position at the top of the stairs. Her bare feet were chilled by the cool, wet grass.

He snapped out of his trance by the force of some powerful maternal magic and was released from the spell. Although his injured head still throbbed, his legs were mobile once again. He turned, clambered up the stairs on all fours and exited the place he had called home for one final time. He collapsed onto the damp lawn at his mother's feet.

Janet stepped over him, lifted the safety latches and slammed down the metal doors with a loud bang. She grabbed a nearby rake and quickly slid it under the metal handles of the bulkhead sealing it shut from the outside like a crypt. She hoped that would be enough to lock her father into the house allowing them the chance to escape.

"*ROT IN FUCKING HELL YOU MONSTER!*" She screamed at the doors. She turned, then bent down to help her son to his feet. She briefly looked him over for further injuries but struggled to see in the dark. Connor looked at his mother with tears in his eyes as she smothered him with the biggest hug of his life. They had never shared an embrace as this filled with such warmth and emotion.

They stood there under the moonlight for no more than a few brief seconds trying their damndest to make-up for twelve years of animosity.

Her hand returned to the back of his head as she was quickly reminded of his cranial injury. They needed to find help but more importantly, they needed to get away from this house. Away from the awful memories that haunted it.

Away from the monster that refused to leave it, even in death. The mother and son retreated.

In the silence of that July night, a small grey mouse scurried along the foundation of the house sniffing around for a morsel of food. It turned as it reached the bulkhead that jutted out towards the backyard. It's beady eyes darted left than right before they spotted something white in the grass. It picked up a fat, squirming maggot to give it a sniff. Disgusted, it dropped the larva as the bulkhead door was shoved forcefully from behind but did not budge. The loud bang startled the mouse who ran off into the dark forest to continue foraging long into the night.

The harmonious chorus of crickets in the grass was briefly accompanied by a low abrasive noise coming from the bulkhead doors. Then the scratches were no more.

- Sixteen -

The pair were in rough shape as they hobbled around the exterior of the house. Janet knew there was no way she could drive in her condition, besides, the keys were somewhere inside the house. With their arms wrapped around each other for support, they limped a short ways down the road under the streetlights until they reached the home of their nearest neighbor.

Connor settled against the wooden railing as Janet walked up the steps of the mobile home and knocked on the screen door.

An elderly woman skeptically peered out from behind a curtain then adjusted her glasses. She flipped on the porch light then immediately swung open the metal door to welcome them in. She sensed something was wrong after she saw the boy was hurt and the mother wore nothing but her nightgown.

"For Heaven's sake, what happened? Are you two okay?" The woman inquired.

Janet, overcome with exhaustion and grief could only manage one word.

"Hospital."

The old woman assumed it was a matter of domestic assault but respectfully refused to ask anymore questions. She shouted to her husband to bring out her spare bathrobe for Janet and a clean towel for Connor. She swiped the keys off the rack by the door then hurried outside into the humid night air to fire up their Oldsmobile. She still wore her fuzzy pink house slippers.

The married couple rode in the front exchanging looks of concern back and forth under the green glow of the dashboard. They didn't say a word to each other but still knew what the other was thinking.

Janet rode behind the driver's seat and Connor laid across the bench resting his head on his mother's lap like a child in need of comfort. Her hand was pressed firmly on the back of his head with the towel to apply pressure to the wound.

As they drove up the road back towards their house, Janet couldn't resist having a look at her old childhood home. She glanced up the driveway towards the house that loomed in the darkness nestled alongside the old cemetery.

She was flooded with memories of her childhood. The rope swing, the nest of baby birds she nursed back to health, climbing trees. Happy memories.

Then she recalled getting yelled at by her parents. The anger and violence. The booze. The name calling. The rape. The betrayal. The abandonment. The overwhelming hopelessness as she ran away from home. That house was a place of evil. What was she thinking moving back there? She was thinking about her son.

For a moment she stiffened with fear as she noticed the lamp in the living room was on. She could see a dark figure standing in the window in front of the lit television. Goosebumps covered her body. Part of her knew without knowing that the t.v. was airing an episode of *M*A*S*H*.

"You can keep the house you sick fucker!" Janet whispered her final words to her father into the glass through gritted teeth.

Janet stared expressionless into the darkness while street lights passed by overhead lighting the inside of the car. A million thoughts ran through her troubled mind while she tried to process what just happened.

As exhaustion set in, she caressed her son's hair with the tips of her fingers and soon she dozed off.

- Seventeen -

A week or so later, Connor had been diagnosed with a
moderate TBI after receiving twelve stitches to the gash
on the back of his head. The neurologist wanted him to
stay in-house for observation to make sure there wasn't
any serious permanent brain damage while Janet worked
on securing new housing at his bedside.

While he was laid up in recovery, Janet was able to
contact her former landlord to make a down payment plus
the security deposit on their old apartment. To her
surprise, one of the nicer apartments on the first floor had
recently become available so they were given first dibs as
former tenants. They had no furniture for the time being,
but it was a place to stay that wasn't the house on Thomas
Hill Road.

She contacted a moving company that agreed to go to
the house to retrieve their belongings including all the
furniture that was left behind by George. The landlord put
in a good word so the movers cut them a deal after he
considered their desperate circumstances. For the time
being, things had started to look up for the Gale family.

Joshua Marsella

One night from his hospital bed, Connor flipped through the channels on the TV that was suspended from the ceiling. Nothing had appealed to him and he wished that he had one of his comic books to read. His mother was sound asleep on the tiny couch. She hadn't had a drink since the night of the attack so even though she was a bit more irritable, she seemed to be getting meaningful sleep for once.

Connor set down the corded TV remote then leaned over to the chair beside his bed. He grabbed his only pair of shorts he had in his possession; The jean shorts he was wearing the night they ran from the house. He patted around then reached into his back pocket and pulled out what he was looking for. An old polaroid.

He pulled the bedside lamp in closer and stared intently at the photograph. It was a picture of young George standing just outside the bamboo hut seemingly after he'd murdered everyone inside. In his bloody hand he held out his trophy necklace. On his face was that eerily charming grin. Connor recognized the smile as being the same one he sees in the bathroom mirror when he brushed his teeth. Connor smiled back at the photo of his father.

He laid his head down on the pillow, rolled over onto his side hugging the polaroid. Soon thereafter, he drifted off to sleep with the photo in his hands

.

On the television, two military helicopters appeared on the screen. They flew over a mountain range then hovered over a medical unit with red crosses on their tent roofs. Gentle guitar plucking and horns of the *M*A*S*H* theme song began to quietly play while the mother and son snoozed away peacefully in the hospital room.

- Epilogue -

A few days later, a large truck with *Dan's Moving Company* written on the side backed down the dirt driveway of the old house next to the Thomas Hill Road Cemetery. Two rugged looking men stepped down out of the cab, swung open the back doors of the box truck, pulled out several blankets and folded up cardboard boxes.

"This is it. Let's get in and get out before dinnertime. I don't want to miss my wife's meatloaf! That shit dries up fast if it has too much time to sit." Dan, a burly bearded middle aged man told his younger co-worker.

"No problem boss! We'll get it done. You know, a little ketchup can go a long way."

"Meh, never liked the stuff. You start in the back bedroom and work your way forward. I'll hit the basement. I'll see if I can bring stuff up out through the bulkhead and save some time. The other guys are on their way. Start by boxing up the small shit. Save the heavy stuff for when the crew gets here."

"You got it! This isn't a bad looking place. I wonder if they're going to sell. With a little work it could easily be flipped. My wife and I are looking for a starter home. Kid's due in January. Kind of creepy being so close to the cemetery though. Ya think?" Craig asked Dan the burly man as he scratched his dry scalp.

"Who knows? I can't figure out why they'd leave a house for a tiny apartment in the first place. Not my problem either. Long as I get paid. Let's move!" The pun was lost on Craig who always lacked a bit in the brains department.

No more words were ever spoken between them. It was time to get to work. Dan went around to the backside of the house and saw a rake jammed into the handles of the bulkhead.

"What the hell? Don't they know these doors lock from the inside? This ain't doing a damn thing!" He removed the rake, jerked open the squeaky metal doors one after the other then descended into the darkness of the basement.

Upstairs, Craig made his way to Janet's former bedroom. He carried a small stack of boxes that were neatly folded flat and a roll of packaging tape. He looked around the room but didn't see much to pack.

"This job should be a piece of cake! Easy money." He unfolded one of the boxes and taped up the bottom. The tape made a loud ripping sound. He kneeled down to check under the bed before he would tackle the closet. There was nothing under there except a shoebox that was tucked away underneath the headboard. Craig shook his head and laughed to himself.

"Women and their shoes. Probably has 20 more pairs of 'em in the closet."

He laid down on his stomach then paused for a moment to listen. He swore he heard a scratching noise. He shook his head in denial, reached under the bed and pulled the box out. He read the writing on top:

HANOI

"Hanoi? What the bloody hell? These ain't no shoes."

Craig opened the lid of the box catching a brief glimpse of George's gruesome war trophy and the balled up t-shirt. He winced in disgust then dropped the box.

"Jesus! Who are these people?"

Janet's clock radio on the nightstand in front of him turned itself on at full volume. Eric Burdon's chalky deep voice screamed out the chorus to *The Animals* hit *We Gotta Get Out of This Place* through the small speakers at the man on the floor.

The closet door swung open, but Craig hadn't noticed.

"*What in the fu-?*"

Craig wasn't given the chance to finish the last sentence he would ever speak nor would he get to hear the cries of his unborn child.

George's rusty bayonet made sure of that.

The End

~ Special Thanks ~

First and foremost I want to thank my wife Aryn who didn't once laugh at me or think I was foolish for wanting to start writing. She has supported me every step of the way. She acted as the first beta reader and offered several suggestions that made their way into the final draft of my story. I love you Aryn!

Next I want to thank my good friend Noah Hersom who enjoys creative writing. He was instrumental in encouraging me to give it a shot. He also volunteered to beta read my story and offered me excellent feedback. You rock!

One more big thank you goes to Ross Jeffery (author of JUNIPER) who reached out to me to volunteer as a beta reader. Ross offered me countless suggestions to improve my overall prose and writing quality. I value his advice and friendship. Thanks bud!

The constructive criticism and feedback I received from my beta readers was absolutely priceless in accomplishing my goal of self publishing my debut novella.

The final thanks goes to everyone that used their hard earned money to buy a copy of my book and their precious time to read my twisted little tale. Thanks for the encouragement and support. I am forever grateful to each and every one of you. Sending love to you all.

- Joshua Marsella -

Manufactured by Amazon.ca
Bolton, ON

15160450R00072